THE BASTARD

Detective Constable Cameron of the Yorkshire County Police was talking to the visiting Detective Inspector from the Metropolitan C.I.D. Cameron said to the younger man:

'Sorry, this is my patch. Mine. This whole bloody division... and that includes this particular hell hole we're driving through.'

They were driving up onto the high moors, and Cameron's Volkswagen was slithering in the heavy snow blizzard. Their task looked to be an easy one, apart from the weather. They were going to arrest a man called Charlie Goodwin for his part in a bank robbery.

Cameron was dead certain they would find their quarry in the remote, empty croft – a tiny dwelling shared by several farmers as a night refuge for shepherds who were caught in bad weather while seeing to their flocks. Cameron was right. They found Goodwin, and Goodwin's instant reaction was murderous and bloody, worse even than Cameron had feared.

Cameron and Goodwin were ancient enemies – a living hatred flashed between them. This is the story of two resourceful and ruthless men, trapped in an isolated croft and trapped too in a vice of mutual hatred.

JOHN WAINWRIGHT

THE BASTARD

HERON BOOKS

Published by Edito-Service S.A., Geneva
by arrangement with Macmillan London Ltd.

© *1976, John Wainwright*
© *1981, Illustration, Edito-Service S.A., Geneva*

Victory comes late,
And is held low to freezing lips
Too rapt with frost
To take it.

How sweet it would have tasted,
Just a drop!
Was God so economical?

Emily Dickinson

CHAPTER ONE

I tell you...

'New Scotland Yard'. Those three words get right up my nostrils. They have done for years.

This coming Christmas will be my nineteenth Christmas, as a cop—my fifth, as a detective constable—and, every Christmas Morning, my sister (whom I love dearly) presents me with a book. And, my being fuzz (and my sister being a woman, with a woman's cockeyed logic), she thinks it appropriate that the book should be a crime yarn.

There is another on the way. The chances are it has already been bought. And, three weeks from today, I'll be pecked on the cheek, and I'll be handed a gaudily wrapped package in which will be one more to add to my collection.

One more Disneyland murder. One more crackbrained solution. I get one at Christmas, I get one at Easter, I get one on my birthday and I get one whenever she feels my sagging morale needs a quick shot of get-up-and-go.

I could start my own lending library ... supposing, that is, I could find enough people eager to read books with mind-blowing titles, on a par with *The Case of the Knotted Knickers*.

And—okay—I am being a little unkind.

Occasionally, she makes a mistake. Occasionally, she buys me a *good* crime yarn. I have (for example) received

7

two Chandlers, over the years ... admittedly, I'd read them both a couple of times but, no matter, they still remain among the handful of books I never lend.

For the rest?

I read them, slot them into my bookshelves, let them gather dust and forget them.

And I have already worked out the odds. The chances are that, this coming Christmas, I will again receive an also-ran. One more splurge of words, strung together by some pen-pusher who wouldn't know a murder enquiry from a hole in the ground. One more kinky amateur sleuth, who will detect the crime while the local gendarmerie are lacing up their boots. Or, conversely, one more high I.Q. mastermind from New Scotland Yard, who will unknot the knots while he straightens his bowtie and flicks the specks from the cuffs of his dinner jacket.

Jesus!

When will these book-boys come out of orbit? When will they tumble that New Scotland Yard is just one more glorified nick ... and, maybe, not even *that*? That the almighty 'Met' is just one more police force and, because it is an uncommonly *big* police force, it carries an uncommonly large number of non-paying passengers? That they are not all 'Charlie Artfuls' or 'Nipper' Reads? That some of them are prize berks?

Like the one riding passenger with me, in this motor car.

He is a detective inspector (no less), and how in hell's name he earned *that* rank before all the talc was dusted clear of his backside only the Almighty, and a handful of very privileged angels, will ever know.

At a pinch, I could be his old man, but I am expected to call him 'sir'.

The hell I will call him 'sir'. I was pushing pavements while he was still carrying a school satchel. I was collecting Misconduct Sheets, for doing my job well, and doing it *my* way, before he used his first razor. When I was in men's surgical, recovering from my first beat-up, the chances are he hadn't yet decided to *be* a copper.

And *I* am expected to call *him* 'sir'.

Let me tell you ... if he doesn't have headaches till then, he'll never need money for aspirins.

What is more, this is my patch and we are two hundred miles north of the room he uses as an office. Which means *I* am king of this particular castle.

His name is ...

We-ell, no matter. He has a name, and I know it, but somebody, somewhere, loves the young pup (otherwise why the rank?) and who am I to tear wings from butterflies? Tomorrow, he will be back with the gilded pavements; he will have touched my life, and blown ... no sweat, and no hazard to the snail-paced advancement of my own career.

So, although the hell I will call him 'sir', I will do him the small favour of keeping his secret. He is merely 'the D.I.' ... and that he is from 'New Scotland Yard' is a big enough cross for him to bear.

I wrestle the wheel of the V.W., the tyres grip on the build-up of snow and the bonnet faces the way I want it to face.

'Rather hairy,' he drawls.

I grunt some sort of reply to this stupid remark.

'With luck, you'll have a white Christmas.'

'Up here,' I say, 'they *always* have a white Christmas. And a white New Year. *And* a white February. With luck, the colour changes in March.'

9

'Really?'

I doubt if he believes me. As a Southerner, he lives in another world. The Tops (which is where we are) can be a miniature Antarctica ... and, most years, *is*. For three months, it takes some of the roughest weather in the U.K.; snowdrifts that bury whole landscapes, and a night and day gale-force blow which bends trees into twisted shapes and plays pitch-and-toss with rotten branches weighing anything up to a couple of hundredweight. And this (early December) is not just the beginning of winter, up here. Here, winter is well into its stride; the frosts are already a nightly nose-biter and, for four weeks now, the sheep have been penned behind bales of straw in the annual fight for survival.

This is a fact of life, up here, on the Tops ... but I doubt if this pampered youth alongside me believes that fact.

I drop the gear lever down into second, and say, 'It's just getting under way.'

'What?'

'Winter. It's flexing its muscles ... no more. Come January, they'll be waiting for clear days, and the chance to drop supplies by helicopter.'

'Every year?'

'Most years.'

I chance taking my eyes from the road, for a second, to glance at him. There is a faint smile of disbelief hanging around his mouth corners.

This young D.I. knows all the answers. He has fought his way through the blizzards of too many Soho porn-shops ... he *knows*!

I let him smile in peace. Less than two miles ahead, we leave the shelter of this car and then (as sure as God invented gobstoppers) he *will* know. When he is an old, old man, he will still be telling his grandchildren all about the smack in the teeth Ma Nature is waiting to give him, when he opens the door of this car.

I have patience. I can bide my time for the sake of a good belly-laugh.

'He won't be there, of course,' he says, very airily.

'Your snout says he might be. My snout says he *is*.'

'Snouts!'

'Speak for yourself,' I growl. 'The lice who whisper sweet nothings in *my* ear don't deliberately lie. Not if they value their dentures.'

'You have something of a reputation.'

'Among the hayseeds,' I agree.

'No ... in your own force. I was warned.'

'Warned?'

'Your boss told my boss, my boss told me. Cameron plays it heavy. Be careful.'

I come back with, 'All that rank you have tucked under your arm? Did you need a briefing, before you met me?'

'Easy, Cameron,' he warns ... but there is a slight shake in his voice.

'Go screw yourself, sonny,' I grunt ... and there is no shake at all, in mine.

I watch the flakes splash, and slide down the wind-screen, before the wipers clear them and, as I slither and skid the car up the one-in-six, I play around with very personal thoughts.

So, my boss has told his boss, has he? Just *what*? That Ray Cameron has a name for slugging it out, with powder-puff tough guys? That, as far as Detective Constable Raymond Cameron is concerned, 'the book' needn't have even been written? That there is a spot on the carpet in front of the chief constable's desk reserved for the said D.C. Cameron and that, fifteen times throughout his service, Cameron has stood on that spot and had his balls chewed off for playing the tearaways at their own game, and by their own rules, and beating blue crap out of 'em?

I can imagine ... I can imagine what *my* boss has told *his* boss.

Half a mile later, he makes what amounts to an apology.

He says, 'Cameron, the last thing I want to do is pull rank.'

'The last thing you're *going* to do is pull rank,' I assure him.

'Meaning?'

I say, 'Sonny, this is my patch. Mine. This whole bloody division ... and that includes this particular hell hole we're driving through. Nineteen years—ever since I tried my first helmet for size—I've chased the rats of this neck of the woods back into their holes. I'm not bragging, boy. It's there on the record. As a uniformed P.C. they were more scared of me than they were of any other copper ... up to, and including, the superintendent. And why? Because I didn't give a damn. Didn't then, and don't now. Any more than they do. Why the hell should we respect the law, when they don't? That's the way I've brought 'em to heel. The *wrong* way ... okay, I've been told *that* more times than I can remember. It's what's held me back. But it's also what's made me cock o' the midden. And, on this midden, nobody pulls rank on Ray Cameron. Nobody!'

'That's something else I was told,' he murmurs.

'You seem to have had a pretty thorough briefing.'

'Fairly extensive,' he admits.

'And Charlie Goodwin?' I ask.

'What about Goodwin?'

'Did they tell you I know him ... personally?'

'You mean you've nicked him? You've...'

'No. I mean we knew each other as kids. Went to the same school. Lived in the same street. Were members of the same teenage gang. And, if you shove your arm deep enough into the sludge, you'll even find blood-ties, of a sort. Cousins ... four or five times removed.'

'Goodwin?'

I say, 'You blokes from the Big Place. They tell me you're great ones for statistics. Now, did you know that more than thirty per cent of all major criminals in the United Kingdom are related to police officers?'

'No.' He blinks, and says, 'No ... I didn't know that.'

'That's not surprising.' I grin. 'I just made it up ... but, as sure as hell, *Goodwin* is. Long years ago, we were buddies.'

'And blood relations?' He compresses his lips as he asks the question.

'Sonny,' I say, 'do me a favour. Forget that part. It's the least important part of all. Maybe that's something my boss *didn't* tell your boss ... that I'd happily nick my own grandmother, if she was bent.'

I can feel his eyes on me, before he mutters, 'That's something I can readily believe.'

'Okay. Believe it ... and stop worrying.'

He stops talking for a while, and lets me concentrate on driving the V.W. along the thickening eiderdown of snow. Except for a Land Rover, I doubt whether a front-mounted engine could make progress across this stuff, but the weight of the old Beetle punches the rear wheels into the softness and, with good tyres (which I've made damn sure are fitted), this bus could give a snow-cat a run for its money. Could be I'm wrong, could be I'm prejudiced ... I happen to like the V.W. Beetle, because it is tough, solid and knows how to fight.

Nevertheless ...

I know this terrain, and I also know the conditions it can drum up, when it really decides to turn nasty, and I have sense enough to be a little worried. The flakes are falling no faster, but they are gradually getting fatter. They are no longer like confetti—which is what they were like when we started to climb—they are more like midget ping-pong balls and, every hundred yards or so, I can feel the tiny shudder as the wheels knock the build-up from the underside of the wings.

If it gets much worse, we have problems.

If a wind decides to join the dance, in earnest, we're in real trouble.

But—what the hell—if I told this overgrown boy scout these things, it wouldn't jell. A surfeit of pigeons around Nelson's Column is *his* idea of a fish-pickle!

I spin the wheel, play toccatas and fugues on the accelerator pedal, and decide to talk a little. To ask a few questions.

I say, 'How come you?'

'I beg your pardon?'

'You ... y'know—why are *you* collecting Charlie Good-win?'

'I'm on the case. Obviously.'

'Forces have their own way of doing things,' I observe.

'I'm sorry. I don't understand.'

'This mob,' I explain. 'When we need somebody for escort duty, we don't always send somebody from the case.'

'No?' He sounds surprised.

'Any banana with nothing better to do. That's who we send.'

'Are you going out of your way to be offensive?' he snaps.

'Christ, no. I'm being *polite*.' I grin at the weather, beyond the nose of the V.W. 'I'm just saying ... not necessarily somebody involved.'

'*I'm* involved.'

'Like I say ... different forces, different ways of working.'

'We think ours is the best way.'

'Snap! So do we.'

'The Met considers....'

'We are,' I growl, 'two hundred miles north of "the Met".'

'I don't see...'

'The New York Police Department carry night-sticks—they also claim to be the world's finest ... *we* don't, and *they* aren't. That's what I'm saying.'

'I still don't see...'

'Stuff the bloody "Met",' I rasp. 'Is that plain enough.'

He says, 'You can't expect me to agree.' And there is no rancour in his voice.

'In these parts, you agree. Or stay quiet.' I blunt the edge of my tone a little, and add, 'We also send two.'

'Escorts?'

'We lose less prisoners that way.'

'I—er—I should have had a colleague.' I have the impression that I have touched a raw spot. That he is embarrassed. He clears his throat, and goes on, 'He—er—he had an accident.'

'Is that a fact? What sort of an accident?'

'It could happen to anybody. At King's Cross ... coming up from the tube.'

15

'I'm interested,' I press.

'He—er ...' He swallows, then blurts out, 'He fell down the escalator. The "up" escalator. He ricked his ankle badly.'

'Oh, my God!'

'It was my decision ... he was only a detective constable. I decided to come on, alone.'

It makes my day. From now on, anything can happen —any cock-up can slide in and smack me in the teeth ... see if *I* care. 'New Scotland Yard'. Gold-plated jacks. All those ding-dong thief-takers the scribblers write about. And they can't even detect their way up a moving staircase!

I laugh so hard, I damn near choke.

'It's not funny,' he snaps.

'Sonny,' I gasp, 'from where I'm sitting, it's hilarious.'

Maybe it's catching. He joins me in a quick chuckle, and says, 'He's a clumsy sod. All feet and legs.'

I regain my breath, and say, 'So, you decided on a solo run?'

'With Goodwin.'

I stop laughing. There is something in this youth's tone which plugs the hilarity gap. Not cockiness, but a certainty. A stupid, foundless, M.P.D. certainty. The brand of 'certainty' that makes aeroplanes try to fly their way through mountains. Suicidal.

'Goodwin,' I say, quietly.

'Assuming he's up here, of course.'

'He'll be up here.'

'So-o ... no real problem.'

'Because it's Charlie Goodwin?'

'He's no tough egg.'

'You have a sworn affidavit, to that effect, of course?'

16

'Oh, for God's sake, Cameron. He was on the raid ... so that makes him as guilty as the other five. But he just stood there. He didn't *do* anything.'

'With a gun in his hand,' I remind him.

'They *all* had guns. The others used them. He didn't. He was the pansy of the team ... obviously.'

'Correct me, if I'm wrong, mister detective inspector,' I say, 'but, as I understand things, the "others"—the tough babies—blew hell out of the ceiling plaster. Right?'

'Scare tactics.'

'The ceiling?' I insist.

'Yes. To frighten the bank customers into submission. Scare tactics.'

'But Charlie didn't?'

'No ... he just stood there.'

I say, 'Will you take it from me that, if Charlie Goodwin had squeezed a trigger, something a damn sight more irreplaceable than plaster of Paris would have been at the receiving end?'

'Are you telling me he's a killer?'

I say, 'I'm telling you he's the only bastard who ever tried to hammer a hole through me ... and the only bastard who almost *did*.'

'That's not the picture we get,' he counters. 'That's not what the bank staff tell us. What the customers say. They all say ...'

'That he just stood there?'

'Quite.' From the corner of my eye, I see him nod.

'So does plastic explosive,' I remind him.

'Eh?'

'It just "stands there". Quiet. Harmless. Not saying a word. Waiting for the right fuse. But, come the right fuse —come the right moment—and it can topple a building.'

17

He takes a deep breath, then says, 'Goodwin?' very gently.

'I know him,' I say. 'I know what he was like ... and he won't have changed.'

'Tell me,' he suggests.

I take it slowly. I concentrate on two things, at the same time. Driving the car, and picking the right words. I pick the words carefully because—and despite the 'New Scotland Yard' tag—this berk is a fellow-cop, I have no wild desire to see him hurt ... at least, not *too* much. He is still damp around the ears, and green around the nostrils, and he is not even from my part of the world but, if I don't wise him, who the hell will? And, if I *don't*, he will simply pull some cackamalarky M.P.D. trick and I'll end up wishing I *had* ... because (believe me) Charlie Goodwin could bone this one and eat him as an apéritif for breakfast.

I say, 'Clear the mind, sonny. Eh? Forget all the bull the would-be heroes have fed you. The customers and the bank staff. Chances are they were shitting themselves, at the time ... they always do. Then, when the fuzz arrive to take statements, they tart the thing up as much as they dare ... to rescue some of their precious self-respect.

'And start with the proposition that Charlie Goodwin is no fairy. You get him back to London, single-handed ... whether you get it, or not, you'll *deserve* the Queen's Police Medal. I *know* the bastard. We ran riot in this district, years back. In our own unique way, we built up a neat little protection racket ... of a sort. Free meals, at most of the fish and chip dumps. At most of the transport cafés. Free entry into the dance halls. The picture houses. Free fags. Free booze. We paid for *nothing* ... almost. Quietly, though. No fuss. No threats. Just a damn good hiding, if anybody stepped too far out of line.'

I glance at him, and say, 'I'm shocking you, maybe?'

'No. It's been known ... in other places.'

'Uhuh. We-ell, it was known in these parts. The two of us—Charlie and me—ran neck-and-neck, all the way across this territory. I was the mouthy one ... you'll have noticed?'

'Yes. I've noticed.'

'But not Charlie. Charlie never said a word. He just let things time themselves ... then exploded.'

'Like plastic explosive?'

'Just like plastic explosive,' I agree.

He mulls over what I have said for a few moments ... and I hope to God he is receiving the message loud and clear.

Then, he says, 'The puzzling thing is ... why?'

'Why what?'

'The force? What you've just described is delinquency ... sheer delinquency.'

'That's one fancy name for it,' I accept.

'So, why the about face? Come to that, how the devil did you get *into* the force, with that background?'

'No previous cons, sonny.' I grin, knowingly, at the windscreen. 'I *deserved* 'em—we both deserved 'em ... I'm not arguing that. But the coppers, in those days ... Dumb. Soft. The uniformed sergeant making the en-quiries—y'know, they trot around to check whether you're a fit and proper person to direct traffic—they don't come thicker. The old lady fed him tea. I fed him fags. After that, he couldn't care less ... I was in.'

'And, despite everything, no previous form?' He sounds a little amazed.

'Let's say we were lucky.'

'That ... or this force really *is* dumb.'

'Was.' I correct the tense. 'These days—this division—not much slips past.'

'Nevertheless...'

All right, Mr. New Scotland Yard detective inspector.
'Nevertheless.'

Nevertheless, I joined the force. I became a copper. I did the perfect horse-switch—the immaculate poacher-to-game-keeper trick—and there has to be a reason.

There has to be a reason ... but I'm damned if I know it!

Maybe, because I lost Charlie. Maybe when he hooked in with the fairground crowd, I became lonely. He was my pal—my equal ... and the only living creature on God's earth I've ever accepted as my equal.

He couldn't out-fight me. He couldn't out-daredevil me. He couldn't out-drink me. But, neither could I out-fight, out-daredevil or out-drink him. If ever two kids reached out for manhood, in double-harness, it was Charlie and me.

I took it bad.

When the swings and the roundabouts left town, and Charlie went with them, I took it just about as bad as I've ever taken anything in my life. He never even mentioned. He just up and left. And, dammit, I wouldn't have known if I hadn't spotted him perched up there, on top of the tarpaulin, on one of the trucks.

I shouted—asked him what the hell he was doing up there ... and he didn't even answer. He grinned, and waved.

Goodbye, Charlie Goodwin.

And, up you, Charlie Goodwin!

Hot irons wouldn't get it out, mate. But I know. I went

on a three-day binge. I was stoned out of my stupid mind, for three solid days.

Why?

Because I was lonely, I reckon. That, and because I'd been at the mucky end of a dirty trick, from the one man alive I'd even half-respected. The one man I'd have trusted to guard my back up to, and including, an earthquake, and he'd pissed off, out of my life, without as much as a 'Kiss my arse, and stuff you, Ray Cameron'.

I was bloody lonely.

And a three-day booze-up didn't help.

I started lonely and sober, and ended lonely and plastered . . . that's all the good it did.

Y'know what, Mr. New Scotland Yard detective inspector? I even contemplated the army. Me! I'd fiddled my way out of conscription . . . just after the war, remember? Reserved occupation. I'd worked that one . . . on paper. But, because I was so damn lonely, I even contemplated joining up as a regular.

How's that for a laugh?

I didn't—hell's bells, I wouldn't have lasted five minutes as a soldier . . . but I joined the force, instead.

Get it?

For mates. To take my mind off things. For something to bloody well do, once Charlie had gone.

Charlie Goodwin . . . the bastard!

You want a reason why I joined the force?

You could say he's the reason . . . Charlie Goodwin.

And now, we're pushing this old car of mine up onto the Tops, in lousy, and worsening, weather, and we're going to arrest him. The man who, maybe more than anybody, is why I'm here, anyway.

Funny?

Ah, well—just as long as you don't think it's going to be easy, Mr. New Scotland Yard detective inspector ... just as long as you don't think anything in this life is easy.

'You haven't answered my question,' he reminds me.

'No. I've better things to do with my breath.'

I pull the V.W. as near to the side of the road as I dare, brake to a halt, but leave the engine running and the fan going. We need as much heat as we can gather, before we hit that weather on the other side of the bodywork.

I light a cigarette, and say, 'Well? What's the plan of action?'

He chews his lip, then says, 'What's this place like?'

It's a fair question. It deserves a full answer.

I say, 'First. We walk, the best part of a mile. It's a muck road ... little more than a cart-track. Even in good weather, only an idiot would risk a car. This weather, you'd need a good tractor, and a sledge. So, we shank it, from here.

'It's a farmhouse. Small, but sheltered ... which means we can get pretty close, without playing Cowboys and Indians. They're all around these parts. In Scotland, you might call 'em crofts. That's what they are ... in effect. Smallholdings. Little farmsteads. The farmer went broke, some years back. They all do ... eventually. Nobody buys these bloody places ... you can't *give* 'em away. So, what happens is this. The neighbouring farmers fit the place out with bare essentials. A bed, a chair, a table. Some grub. Wood and coal. Then—if they're caught in a sudden hill mist, they've a shelter. Communal, you might say. A sort of glorified hidey-hole, till the weather breaks. These places have saved more lives than *that*. Come sheep-gathering, and they all know where there's shelter if it's needed.

Fell-walkers use 'em, too ... if they're caught with their pants down.

'That's where Goodwin is. Up there, in a farmstead. Waiting till the heat cools, and he can make a run for it.'

'You *know* that?'

'Aye.' I nod. 'He's been seen. And I've been told. And smoke's been seen coming from the chimney.' I growl, 'Sonny, you wouldn't catch me out in this lot ... not unless I was bloody sure.'

'Front door? Back door? Windows?' he asks. 'Just in case he tries to make a run for it.'

'In *this* weather?' I scoff.

'It's been known.'

'All right.' I humour him. 'Front door *and* back door. Two rooms upstairs. Two rooms downstairs. The downstairs rooms ... living room and scullery. No halls ... nothing fancy, like that. The front door leads straight into the living room. The back door to the scullery. The bed'll be downstairs. Nothing upstairs ... they don't go in for civilised flippery, when it's a matter of simple survival. He'll be using the one room. Lay your life on it.'

'Windows?' he asks.

'Sash-type. Small-paned. You can forget the windows. They'll be stuck, tighter than a virgin's fanny ... they always *are*. He'll need an axe—summat like that—to smash his way out of the windows.'

'All right. Front door, back door. You take the back— I'll take the front ... standard procedure.'

'Copybook,' I murmur.

'That's *why* it's copybook.'

'Except...'

'What?'

I move my shoulders, and grunt, 'He *isn't* ... that's all.'

23

For the first time, he puts a touch of D.I. bite into his tone, as he says, 'Cameron. Don't fall in love with the hound. Eh? He was your pal ... *once*. No more. Not today. Today, he's a bank hold-up man, and you're a copper.'

'I don't need reminding, sonny,' I growl.

'That's reassuring.'

I show him the contempt I feel for jumped-up nobodies, screw out the cigarette, switch off the fan and turn off the ignition.

I say, 'Let's go, Mr. detective inspector. Let's see how *this* climate grabs you.'

CHAPTER TWO

I'm dressed for it. I'm wearing an extra pullover, a scarf, a heavy, belted crombie, a hat and wool-lined leather gloves. So what? Within ten minutes of leaving the car, the temperature had worked its way through, and the cold was already bone-deep.

The D.I.? His lightweight, mohair overcoat looks a little like wet cardboard. He is hatless and gloveless, and he is wearing a skullcap of snow which melts and drips down his face, and down the back of his neck. His complexion has turned into one of those colours the arty-arty crowd go ga-ga about ... a mottled, duck-egg blue.

Christ only knows how cold *he* feels.

This is one of those freak, early December days; a freak day, even up here on the Tops.

The wind has suddenly wound itself up to a steady fifty knots, and the snow is riding it, all the way down. We are having to walk backward, or be half-blinded, and the limit of our visibility—along the way we've already come—is not much more than thirty feet.

I swear ... we are both certifiable lunatics!

I lead the way (if you can call stumbling backwards 'leading the way') and some of the drifts are already knee-deep. Maybe I am still wearing shoes—I wouldn't know ... I can't see them for padded snow and, sure as hell, I can't *feel* them. I wouldn't even bet too much money that I'm still wearing *feet*.

I risk a quick squint, up at where the sky should be, but the sky isn't there any more. Only snow. Spinning, dancing, flying flakes which, if you watch them long enough, make you dizzy.

I keep the dry-stone wall on my right, shove my gloved hands deeper into the pockets of the crombie, and push one leg, then the other, backwards. It is one hell of a way of making progress.

I wait for the old tractor shed to come up and, when we reach it, I duck inside. Most of the roof has gone, but the walls give some sort of shelter from the wind and the driving white stuff.

I grab the D.I., as he staggers past, and drag him into what little shield there is.

He looks like a half-drowned cat. He is shivering, and he flaps his arms across his chest to bring back some of his body-warmth.

We have to shout a little, to make ourselves heard above the wind.

'A quick in-and-out,' I bawl.

'What's that?'

'Grab him, and away. Back to the car. We haven't too much time.'

'No. No ... I realise that.'

'So, don't tool around with Official Cautions, and such-like. That damn car might be under a drift already.'

'I know.' He moves his head a little, stops the draught from a hand-sized hole in the broken stonework of the wall and winces as the cold slices across his face. He gasps, 'Jesus! Is it *always* like this, up here?'

'We've picked a bad day.'

I feel for the inside pocket of my jacket, and pull out the blackjack. I don't carry truncheons, or handcuffs. I carry a blackjack and a figure-eight 'nipper'. The black-jack is a custom-made weapon; ten inches of spring-steel, leather-bound and with a lead-weighted end. I slip the thong over my gloved right hand, and curl my fingers around the grip.

'Those damn things are illegal,' he shouts.

'People keep telling me.'

'Don't use it, unless you have to.'

'No ... I never do.'

'What's that?'

'Unless I have to.'

I doubt if he hears me.

He shouts, 'How far, yet?'

'Less than fifty yards.' I point the blackjack along the wall, parallel to the lane we've just backed our way along. 'The weather's rough, but it's on our side. We'll be there, before he sees us ... even if he's watching for trouble.'

'In this stuff?'

'He's a lot to lose.'

'Could be,' he concedes, then yells, 'Okay. From here, I go first. Keep close. And we face the way we're going.'

I nod agreement, and we duck out into the weather.

This young pup. Could be I have been subjecting him to some slight slander. He surprises me a little. He has more spunk than I gave him credit for; he takes this blow—snow, and all—and pushes his way forward at a speed I have to work at to equal.

We are both bent damn near double, and our legs are like pistons as we fight a way through this 'Tops Special' but, in less than five minutes, we are leaning with our backs to the wall, at each side of the closed door, and pulling in breath.

The farmhouse gives some shelter from the blast, and

27

we watch each other across the doorway as we wait for the next move.

He nods, and I turn to plough my way towards the back of the house.

And then, the young idiot does something stupid.

He can't wait. Maybe he is worried about the car. Maybe the cold has screwed his decision-making apparatus to hell. Maybe anything.

Whatever ... he can't wait.

As I duck under the window, I hear him kicking at the closed door.

I turn as he yells, 'Police! Open up, Goodwin. We know you're there.'

Then comes the roar of a shotgun, one of the lower door panels is blasted to blazes and the D.I. screams as the shot takes him below the knees, punches his legs back and tips him forward, so he smacks the door with his face.

He lies there, bleeding all over the beautiful snow, biting his teeth to keep back the sound of pain and looking across at me. Sorrowfully. Pleadingly. Almost apologetically.

'Great,' I snarl, savagely. 'That's *all* we needed.'

But my mind is working.

That blast ... it had the sound of a double-barrel blast. Which means we are not up against a repeater. Which means Charlie has to re-load ... which, in turn, takes time.

Okay—he has now had time ... but there is another door.

The back doors to these farmsteads are never locked. They are never bolted. Who the hell comes all this way out to steal? It's part of the regular routine, in these parts. Don't lock doors ... it's a silent insult to your neighbour. And—another thing—you might even *need* a neigh-

bour in a hurry. So, why lock him out? And—finally—
the privy to these dumps is a hole in the ground, at the
back of the house so, in case the urge of nature becomes
a little hectic, the back door doesn't even *have* a lock.
Or even a bolt. Just a 'sneck' ... and, if you don't know
what a 'sneck' is, who cares?

So-o, keep your legs tightly crossed, Charlie Goodwin,
otherwise you just *might* be out-smarted.

I crawl my way along the front of the house, along the
side and along the back. At the back, I take the full
force of the weather and, to keep to the wall, I have to
burrow my way through one continuous drift. It isn't nice,
and my temper suffers.

Nor does it soothe my feathers to know that there is the
possibility of a twelve-bore being shoved through a window, prior to it coughing shot in my general direction.

Charlie, boy ... when I get to within reaching distance,
you're going to know I've arrived!

I reach the back door. I stand to one side, and work my
feet into some sort of grip in the snow. I bend into a sprint
position, glance up at the sneck and take a couple of deep
breaths.

Then, I do an encore to the front door concerto.

I lean forward, hammer the bottom panels with the
blackjack and bawl, 'Come on, Goodwin. This is the tram
terminus. This is the end of the ride.'

And he lets fly. Both barrels—I think ... I *hope*. A foot-
wide hole of splintered woodwork becomes part of the
bottom half of the door.

I grab for the sneck, and hit the door with my shoulder.
The door flies open and, on its way, belts the barrels of
the twelve-bore which Charlie has already broken, prior to
feeding more cartridges into the breech. It damn near

knocks the shotgun out of his grip, and makes him stagger back a pace.

I go in, like a wild bull, with the blackjack already back for the swing. He tries to fend it off ... but he is a week too slow.

I murmur, 'Happy birthday, Charlie,' as the leaded end lands across the side of his skull and blows every fuse in his circuit.

I collect the shotgun, toss it into the front room, and kick the two new cartridges he was holding out of harm's way, under the sink. I follow the shotgun, open the front door and give my undivided attention to the wounded warrior.

He has hauled himself into a sitting position, against the wall alongside the door, and the effort has left snail-trails of blood in the snow and done nothing at all to ease the pain.

I say, 'This isn't guaranteed to make you laugh ... but it's the quickest way.'

I grab a handful of his mohair overcoat, at the back of the neck, drag him inside, lean him against the wall, along-side the fireplace, then ask, 'Do you carry handcuffs, sonny?'

'Is he—is he ...?'

'He's in Dreamland. Answer the question. Handcuffs?'

'In—in my hip pocket,' he gasps.

I feel around the back of him, locate the handcuffs, remove the key and return to the scullery.

Charlie is still asleep, but Charlie will not sleep forever and, when Charlie wakes up, Charlie is likely to be good and mad.

So-o ...

I clip one cuff onto his right wrist, drag him to the sink,

then link him so he is embracing the wrought-iron pipe which feeds the pump ... and, unless he can bend iron and pull a wall down, without making noise, he is safe.

A thought strikes me. Why the hell should Charlie be the odd man out? Why the hell should the D.I. and I be cold and wet, while Charlie stays warm and dry? I can think of no good reason.

There is a two-gallon zinc bucket under the sink. I work the pump and fill the bucket with water. Water straight from a *very* deep well. Water so cold, it damn near burns.

I pour the water over Charlie. Slowly. The head, the shoulders and the chest. I don't waste a drop. He takes the full two gallons, and it soaks him to the skin.

It also brings him round and, after an initial grunt, he looks up and recognition flickers across his eyes.

I lower the bucket, and growl, 'Yeah ... it's me, Charlie. And a word of advice. I have work to do in the other room. One pip out of you, and I'll be back here ... and I'll boot your ribs in, just for laughs. You may have gone soft over the years, buddy-buddy. I wouldn't know. Me? I've hardened up ... considerably. I'll take you in mangled —I'll take you in dead, if necessary—so, if you want to stay upright, be good.'

Back in the front room, I check on what I have to work with.

There is a collapsible iron bed, in one corner, complete with palliasse, pillows and blankets. There is a plain, deal-topped table and a couple of broken-down chairs. There is also a primus stove. The fire is lit, and there is a supply of logs and some coal in the corner of the room opposite the bed.

There is a ceiling-high cupboard alongside the fireplace

and, when I open the doors, I am pleasantly surprised. We're not likely to starve to death ... and (but, of course, knowing Charlie) there is booze on the bottom shelf.

Things could be one hell of a lot worse.

I strip off my hat, gloves, crombie and shoes and arrange them in front of the hearth. I feed more logs onto the fire, then slip the blackjack from my wrist and place it, in a handy position, on the broken mantelshelf.

Then, I turn my attention to the D.I.

I don't pull punches.

I say, 'First Aid, sonny. That's all I know. That, plus common sense. It has to hurt—that goes without saying ... but I'm the nearest you're going to get to a medic for some time. Okay?'

'Okay.' He nods, and tries to grin ... and that takes some guts.

First the mohair overcoat, then the jacket. Then, very carefully, the shoes and socks; they are snow-soaked, bloodstained and very messy.

Then I pull the blankets from the bed. When this little lot is over, sonny-boy is likely to need as much warmth as possible, to counter the shock. And dry blankets—as opposed to wet blankets—are what he is going to be glad of.

Then comes the waltz.

We grab each other, and I half-carry, half-drag him to the bed, and lower him onto the palliasse. I ease him into a straight-out position, and he grunts as the pain drives its knives home ... and that it drives them deep can be seen by the sweat which trickles down his chalk-white face.

'Relax, sonny,' I say. 'That's one bad part over. I'll be back.'

I go into the scullery to collect the bucket, pump about six inches of water into it, and boot Charlie in the side, as a reminder, before I return to the main room.

After that, there is a wait, until the primus brings the water to the boil.

There is a decision to be made but, truth to tell, I have almost made it.

Those pellets. They collected muck from the door, on their way to sonny-boy's legs, and they weren't clinically clean when they left the twelve-bore. There is a lot of filth, and a lot of dirty lead, in that mushed-up flesh and (from what First Aid garbage the force has rammed down my throat) lead-poisoning is a damn sight easier to catch than a cold in the head.

Those pellets have to come out ... fast.

Okay—I could maybe leave the D.I. here, make for the car and hare to civilisation, for help. But that would mean leaving the New Scotland Yard berk here, with Charlie. And, I know Charlie. The bastard wouldn't be safe in a *cage*; he'd come up with *something* ... and, for the second time in my life, I'd have egg-yolk running down my face.

I'm staying.

Which means the decision doesn't really have to be made ... the circumstances have made it for me.

I am a smoker. I smoke cigarettes, and I also smoke a pipe. This means I have a 'pipe-smoker's pocket knife'; a knife with a blade, a reamer and a spike, with which to poke out the dottle from the bowl of the pipe. I have already decided ... the spike is what I am going to use.

I take out the pocket knife, open up the spike and show it to the D.I.

I say, 'That's the gadget, sonny. Those lead pellets have to come out ... that's the first job. They *have* to come out. And this glorified darning-needle is the best I can offer. It's not too clean. The truth is, it's filthy. But, if I boil it for ten minutes, that should kill *something*.'

He nods, but doesn't say anything.

I figure he's scared, but won't show it. So, what if he *is* scared? Who the hell *wouldn't* be scared at the prospect of do-it-yourself surgery with a piece of cheap steel that was meant to strip carbon from briar?

I close the spike, open out the blade, and start cutting away his trousers. Starting from the bottom, I open up the seams of each leg. Then, I unfasten his belt and ease the material away from his smashed calves.

I have seen bigger messes ... but not many. Two twelve-bore cartridges can make a god-awful mess of *anything*. But there is a lot of blood, and the first thing is to clear the gore and see just exactly *what* he has left below the knee-caps.

I fish a newly-laundered handkerchief from my jacket pocket, shake it out and go into the scullery. On a shelf, above the sink, I find a pan which, at least, *looks* clean. I rinse it under the pump, then three-quarters fill it with 'clean' water from the pump.

Charlie twists around, to watch, but keeps his mouth zipped.

He, too, is suffering a certain amount of hurt. The side of his head and face is starting to swell and colour, where it stopped the blackjack.

Screw Charlie!

Were it not for Charlie, I'd be roasting my backside against a radiator, in the C.I.D. office.

Back in the main room, I close the blade of the pocket

knife, open the spike and drop the knife into the boiling water on the primus.

Then, I start sponging. It is slow work and, as far as the D.I. is concerned, pretty painful work. I need four fresh pans of water before I have a clear view of the damage ... and, although it is not as bad as I first thought, it is bad enough.

One bone in the left leg is broken ... that, for sure. Could be there is also a broken bone in the right leg. I lack X-ray eyes, so I can't be sure, but I wouldn't be too surprised. The flesh on both legs is chewed, as only a close-range shotgun blast can chew flesh and, at a guess, there is at least a dozen pellets in among the mush. Some of them very deep-bedded.

I eye the mess, and silently curse Charlie in plain and fancy language.

I go to the cupboard, alongside the fireplace, and find a cup and a half-full bottle of Scotch. I fill the cup, and hold it out to the D.I.

He moistens his lips, and says, 'I can take it, without...'

'Maybe. But, I *can't*,' I say, harshly. 'I'm a working jack, not a sawbones. When I start probing around, in that lot, I want to be sure—as sure as I can be—that at least one of us isn't likely to puke all over the place. Savvy?'

He nods, and says, 'Okay. Point taken.'

He drinks at the whisky, and the cup rattles against his teeth.

I use the handkerchief to lift the bucket from the primus, then yank both pullovers clear of my head and roll up my shirt sleeves. I figure I, too, could do with a quick slug of liquid courage and tip the bottle to my lips, then into the scullery for some soap and back to shove my hands into the bucket. The water is damn near hot enough to scald but, no matter, I have watched enough hospital movies to know that clean hands go with operating theatres.

Christ ... operating theatres!

I fish the knife from the bucket, go back to the pump and rinse all the soap from my hands, wrists and the knife then, because I'm scared of drying things on filthy cloth, I return to the fire and let the warmth do the drying for me.

And, okay, maybe I am doing all the wrong things but, in a situation like this, what the hell are the *right* things.

I take a few lungsful of air and walk to the bed.

The D.I. looks up at me and smiles—and could be it is a drunk's smile ... I certainly hope so.

I nod at his middle, and crack, 'Candy-striped underpants. Only a bloody Met copper would *dare*.' Then, I growl, 'Hold tight, sonny. Here it comes.'

Twenty minutes later it is all over. Twenty of the lousiest minutes.of my whole life ... and definitely *the* lousiest minutes of *his*.

I have winkled fifteen tiny pieces of lead from his legs. Fifteen times—and more—I have driven this damn spike into his flesh, and poked around feeling for what shouldn't be there. Deep and bloody. Crazy surgery no man should have to perform, and no man should have to suffer. And (God help me) not a peep out of the D.I. Not a murmur. Towards the end, I had to go down into the flesh, and he jerked and the spike snagged against the edge of the broken bone. I almost threw up ... but it was necessary, and that sudden rip of extra pain turned out his lights.

He didn't feel the last few come out ... and, for that, I give thanks.

And now?

I throw the blood-soaked knife into a corner, and plunge my stained hands into the cooled water of the bucket. I dry my hands, by wiping them against the side of my trousers, then grab the whisky bottle and pour golden warmth down my throat.

Could be, I've killed him. I wouldn't know. I wouldn't be too surprised. The human frame can take only so much shock, before it opts out ... and the shock *his* frame has taken has been both hard and long. Maybe he'll regain consciousness. Maybe not. Who the hell cares, any-way?

Some young pup, from The Big City, and they dress him in man-sized authority and send him on a man-sized job. What the hell else, but that he gets hurt? What the hell *else*?

I hunt around.

There is a cheap suitcase, under the bed. Charlie meant to stay here a few days; there is clothing and, among the clothing, there is a brand new shirt, still in its cellophane wrapper. And some underclothes, which are clean and un-soiled.

I rip a door from the cupboard and, with the heel of my shoe, splinter it into lengths with which to make some kind of splint. I pad the mangled flesh with the under-clothes. I tear the shirt into strips and, with the strips, bind both legs together with a makeshift splint down each side. I tie the material tight up to, and above, the knees.

Then I settle his head on the pillow, and cover him with the blankets.

His face is quite relaxed. He looks like a pale child, in a deep sleep ... and I wish this damn 'boss' he has men-tioned could see him now!

I use the rest of the clothes from the suitcase as a bung to close the hole in the door. Then I toss a couple of logs on the fire, sit on one of the chairs, and light a cigarette.

CHAPTER THREE

We have everything. All we need is some hairy-kneed scoutmaster, two quick choruses of *Under The Spreading Chestnut Tree* and a knot-tying competition.

Other than that, we have everything.

The D.I. is back from The Land of Dreams. My guess is that he is hurting like hell but, apart from a complexion Marley's ghost might envy, he is keeping the pain under wraps.

Charlie, too, is hurting ... but who wants to know? One side of his face is swollen, and has all the colours of a Turner seascape, and one of his eyes is closed. But, at least, he is out of the scullery. I have hauled him into the main room and shackled him to the ironwork of the bed. Once—about half an hour ago—he jerked at the cuffs, when my back was turned, and the movement brought a hiss of agony from the D.I. I didn't argue. I didn't tell the bastard what I *might* do, if he misbehaved himself. I kicked him in the guts—hard ... and, since then, he has moved very carefully.

So far, Charlie has fired off more twelve-bore cartridges than he has words. But that's okay. That's Charlie. That is how talkative he is ... and always was.

Me?

I am the busy little hausfrau. I am 'home-making' for these two creeps. Dusk arrived some time ago, but a Tilley lamp is giving light enough to shame most electric bulbs.

39

The fire is well stoked and, whatever else, we won't freeze to death. And now I am heating tinned soup, in the pan, on the primus.

We are becoming very domesticated.

Outside, the snow has eased a little ... maybe.

The wind has dropped a little ... again, maybe.

It matters not too much ... we are all three here for the night.

The soup begins to boil, and climbs up the pan. I take the pan from the blue flame of the primus and divide it into two bowls and the can from which I poured it. I hand one of the bowls to the D.I. and place the can on the flagstoned floor, within reach of Charlie.

I go to the cupboard, and tear open a packet of crackers.

I say, 'No bread, folks. Biscuits—or nothing ... and be glad.'

As I hand him a couple of crackers, the D.I. says, 'Thanks, Cameron. You'd make somebody a fine wife.'

Charlie takes his biscuits, without a word, reaches out to lift the can of hot soup and jerks his hand from the near-boiling-point metal.

'Please yourself,' I growl. 'That's what you're drinking it from. And, Charlie—for all I care—you can tip it onto the floor and lick it up.'

His face stays swollen and deadpan, but the eye which is open hands me a look which is a warning. Since we arrived, I have hurt his pride and he is storing up the various points to be settled. Given the chance—given *half* a chance—and the scales will be weighed a little less heavily on my side.

I should worry!

The day Charlie Goodwin can take *me* apart will be a day when the moon outshines the sun.

We drink soup and chew biscuits, and the D.I. feels like talking.

He says, 'Tomorrow, if the snow stops, they should be able to land a chopper ... don't you think?'

'If they can guess where we are,' I agree, gruffly.

'I'm sorry...' His face puts on a puzzled look. '*I* didn't tell anybody.'

'Oh!'

'Did *you*?'

'No. I didn't know.'

'So-o.' I shrug. 'They'll be out looking. But I doubt if they'll find.'

He begins, 'Surely to God you told somebody where...'

'Why the hell should I?'

'It's no great secret. Your boss...'

'My boss,' I snap, 'knows what I tell him. Which isn't much. I'm not the trusting type, sonny. You speak for yourself ... but, up here, they claw their way to the top of the dung-heap on the backs of other men's necks. But not *mine*.'

'Well, of all the idiotic...'

'I didn't let this bastard shoot my legs from under me. If we're comparing idiocies, sling that in the pot, too.'

It quietens him, like a slap in the face. It was meant to. I don't like being called an idiot ... maybe because I've *been* an idiot too many times.

We drink soup and chew biscuits and, gradually, the sun peeks through again and he looks a little less like a kid who has had his backside tanned for something he hasn't done.

'They'll see the smoke,' he says, after a while.

'Could be,' I grunt.

'Once the snow stops. They'll have a chopper out, look-

ing for us. They'll spot the smoke from the chimney ...
then they'll get us out.'

'Maybe.'

'You don't sound too sure.'

'Okay.' I finish my soup and munch the last of my
biscuits as I rip the wick from his candle. 'You want the
truth about Father Christmas? I'll give it. This is a hick
force, sonny. Good ... but without too many frills. So-o,
the first problem is the helicopter. We don't have one,
and the rate-payers don't like parting with money till
they're sure. Maybe tomorrow. Maybe not. Maybe the
day *after* tomorrow ... maybe the day after *that*. Eventually, they'll hire one. Eventually! But they're going to
be damn sure we can't get back under our own power
before they do.

'And—when they do, when they're up there, scanning
for signs of life—what are they going to see? A lot of
white stuff ... that's all. Some farmhouses. Some—here,
and there ... and most of 'em with smoke coming from
their chimneys. And why? Because central heating is
counted a little "pansy" in these parts.'

'I can see that. But this place—they'll know it's ...'

'They'll know nothing. Half these damn places aren't
even on the map. The others? A thing to remember, Mr.
detective inspector. When you use the term "local knowledge", around here, you're not talking about something
you can read up in a book. It means *knowing* ... finding
out, the hard way. I doubt if another copper in this
division knows about this place. Whether it's still being
worked, or not. Whether it's even *here* ... and, if it is,
whether it should be. Okay, come tomorrow—if the
weather clears a little—we'll shove something outside. A
flag maybe. Maybe a fire ... something. To give some

wandering chopper a hint that we're up here.'

'Oh. I see.'

'Tough?' I give him a sardonic smile, with the question.

He hesitates, then says, 'Unexpected,' in a very meaningful tone.

'Isn't everything?' I glance at Charlie, and add, 'He didn't "expect" us, for example. Sure as hell, he didn't expect *me.*'

Charlie nurses the soup can, and makes believe he hasn't heard.

'You think a few days, then?' says the D.I. quietly. A little sadly.

'I'd say,' I agree, with a nod. 'That way, nobody gets disappointed.'

'Quite.' His voice is soft, and he looks down the bed, to where the blankets cover his smashed legs, sighs, then repeats, 'Quite.'

'We'll make it, sonny,' I growl. 'All that "New Scotland Yard" stuff. All that whalebone and iron filings ... you'll breeze through it.'

He chuckles, gently, but the chuckle is overloaded with something not far from self-abasement.

Then, he looks across at me, and says, 'Your wife? Won't *she* be worried?'

No, Mr. New Scotland Yard detective inspector, my wife will not be worried.

By this time, she will be in bed. A little dope—a little soft talk—and, in no time at all, she will be dreaming.

God in his glory knows what the hell she dreams. Or even if she dreams. But, they are not nightmares ... and for that small mercy I am thankful. What dreams she

43

*might enjoy are gentle dreams, because she is a gentle
woman. Her sickness is a burden she, herself, does not
have to hump around on her back. She is unaware of it.
She is kind—her needs are catered for, by kind people—
therefore, she lives in a world of perpetual kindness.*

A false world.

*In her world, there is no snow. There is no cold, and
no wind. There are no guns and no villains. There is
neither law, nor lawlessness, therefore coppers do not exist.
The sour taste of defeat has been rinsed from her mouth.
The bile of ineffectual anger no longer burns her guts.
She is incapable of hatred. Equally, she is incapable of
loving. She is incapable ... period.*

*A false world ... if only because it is a happy world.
And a happy world, because unhappiness is refused entry.*

Therefore, my wife won't be worried.

*Whether I return home, or not—whether I live or die ...
she won't even know.*

*My sister. She won't worry ... I've spent too many
nights on the tiles for her to lose any sleep.*

*I carry the curse of every 'loner'. There are times when
insularity brings its own problems.*

Charlie says something.

We have been relaxing, for a while, each nursing his
own thoughts. The D.I. and I have been soothing those
thoughts with cigarette smoke. We have warmth from the
fire and light from the Tilley. All we need is patience ...
and, could be, that is a commodity we are a little short
of.

Charlie wants something he hasn't got.

He says, 'Am I allowed to smoke?'

His swollen face makes the words slightly mumbling,

but the voice is the same old voice. It has a hoarse quality —like a creaking hinge which isn't used often ... which needs either usage, or oil. Charlie's voice is like such a hinge. Who knows? Perhaps for the same reason ... because he doesn't use it much.

And now, he says, 'Am I allowed to smoke?'

'Anything, Charlie,' I come back with, in a flat voice. 'For me, you can roll onto the fire and burn. It's your choice.'

'Easy Cameron.' The D.I. disapproves of such talk. 'Give him a cigarette. Give him one of mine.'

'*You* give him one. The effort might remind you of what he's done to your legs.'

'For God's sake, Cameron!'

'You're feeling magnanimous, sonny. Not me. I give creeps like this nothing. Nothing!'

Charlie listens to the exchange and, with his damaged face, smiles a sly, lopsided smile. He has found one more sucker ... and he knows it.

The D.I. says, 'Okay, Goodwin. Take one from my packet.'

As I stand up from the chair, I snap, 'Hold it, Charlie. Keep your arse parked on that floor. *I* don't trust you upright, even if *he* does.'

It's the lesser of two evils. A choice between giving the bastard an edge, or doing a slight personal climb-down. I climb down, take the Met boy's cigarettes from the side of the bed, toss one to Charlie, then drop matches onto the flagstones, within his reach. And, as he lights up, I watch him, cat-and-mouse keen and with my hand resting on the mantelpiece, within reach of the blackjack.

This animal I trust ... about as far as I can push Buckingham Palace.

Charlie nods his thanks to the D.I., throws the matches back onto the bed and inhales cigarette smoke.

I relax a little, and fold myself onto the chair once more.

The D.I. gives a sad little smile, and says, 'Why?'

'Forget it,' I mutter.

'All that hatred.'

'Uhuh ... enough for us both.'

'But *why*?'

I give the D.I. a hard look, and say, 'You have a surprisingly short memory.'

'That he's under arrest? No ... I haven't forgotten.'

'That he's committed armed robbery. That, a few feet higher, and he'd have been a cop-killer.'

'It can be argued that he's still innocent ... that he hasn't yet stood trial.'

'And the legs?' I ask, with some curiosity.

'I've no intention of handing him a defence, on a plate.'

'Y'know, sonny,' I muse, 'you're like every other half-baked intellectual who joins the police force. You want it coming and going. "Innocent until proved guilty" ... how the hell guilty he is. Charlie, here. We both know he was in on a bank stick-up. That he sent two parcels of buck-shot into your legs. We both *know* that. And, if some Toc-H jury finds him "Not Guilty", that won't prove he *didn't* ... it'll only prove that it was a Toc-H jury.'

'I've heard the argument.'

'It's no argument. It's a basic fact of policing.'

'I think not.'

'Okay—you "think not",' I mock. 'That's one reason why you're flat on your back, crippled. Me? I remember Charlie. Twenty years ago—longer ... and he was riding

46

out of my life, on the back of a dismantled roundabout. He was a bastard then. He's still a bastard. He's as guilty as hell ... of everything! That's why *I'm* not flat on *my* back.'

'It could also be why you're still a detective constable,' says the D.I., sadly. 'You could have gone higher.'

'You haven't known me long.'

'I think so. Long enough to judge.'

Charlie says, 'The fairground didn't last long.'

'Who wants to know?' I snarl.

'*I* want to know.' The D.I. holds up a hand, as I start to say something. 'The three of us. We're here ... whether we like it, or not. We'll have a truce. We'll talk, even if it's only to pass the time. But some subjects are forbidden. Anything to do with the hold-up. Anything to do with my legs. Other than that, the conversation's wide open.'

'You're crazy,' I growl.

The D.I. ignores my opinion, looks at Charlie, nods and says, 'The fairground? Which fairground?'

Charlie glances up at me and, as far as his damaged face will allow, grins.

The thought strikes me. I am fighting two of them. An animal, and an idiot. And, although the idiot doesn't recognise the animal, the animal recognises the idiot ... which is one way of admitting that I have trouble on my hands.

You think not? You think, maybe, that I am exaggerating? That the D.I. is right, and I am wrong?

You have my word; there are some men who are rotten, from the skin inwards. All the way through to the marrow of their bones. Rotten ... to every last cell in their body.

Not many. Most people go through life without even meeting them. But they're around.

And Charlie is one of them.

For the first time in my life I hear protracted talk from Charlie. In that rusty-hinge of a voice of his, he spins a neat yarn. I don't doubt that he tells the truth—why the hell shouldn't he?—but, if so, he tells it for a purpose. To smooth his way into the confidence of this idiot detective inspector; like a trickster, setting the sucker up for the big sell ... only, with Charlie, it is going to be something a damn sight more lethal than any sell.

And the D.I. listens, and is interested.

Me?

I make-believe not to listen ... but I can't help hearing.

The fairground gaff lasted less than six months.

It ended at a town in Nottinghamshire. Charlie and his mates were riggers-cum-bouncers and, one Saturday night, the heavies from some other outfit started to throw muscle. There was a shindig, and the police were called in to break things up. A bunch of them spent a night in the cells, and were hauled in front of the beak, next morning, to face a mixture of Breach of the Peace and G.B.H. charges. Charlie was fined and bound over but, when he walked out of the court-house, he found the fair had moved on.

He odd-jobbed from meal to meal for a fortnight or so, then he saw a poster. A circus was visiting a neighbouring town.

One of the hand-to-mouth, tented circuses. A one- two-three-night stand, family job, where the budget is so tight a rise in the price of sawdust can bring bankruptcy.

Charlie hitched to the neighbouring town, found the site and talked himself into the job of Man Friday for a starvation wage.

For two years, he did everything. Helped with the canvas, fed the animals, wore clown's outfits, collected the tickets, drove the tractor, sold the ices ... everything! He lived rough. His bed was in the back of one of the trucks. He even shared horse-meat with the trio of cats which made up the animal act.

But he did something else ... he breathed in 'circus'.

The seven-day-a-week, dawn-till-dusk back-break which has nothing whatever to do with money, or wages. The dulled spangles were still spangles. The torn tights were still tights. And, if the music came from a record, it didn't matter ... it was still 'circus music'.

Charlie *became* 'circus'.

At the end of two years, he had an ambition. He wanted to be a flyer. The élite of the ring; one of a trapeze group, earning top billing in the great circuses of the world.

And Charlie was no slouch, once he'd made up his mind. He was already known, within the tight community of the caravan folk, and friends of friends of friends arranged for him to move to Switzerland and the Circus Knie.

He was still a menial, but he had a base and, during his first year with Knie, he worked towards his goal.

He was the driving force behind the formation of a group. First a 'catcher'; a middle-aged man who'd hung from the catching bar of a recently disbanded act; a man who'd regularly caught two-and-a-half in performances and, sometimes, triples in practice. This man—this catcher —was to be the foundation, upon which Charlie could build an act. The old hand, who knew the secrets of timing and swing ... and who was prepared to pass those secrets onto young and eager learners.

The catcher was a Pole, by birth, but international as

far as his art was concerned. A slow-spoken, careful man who had seen maiming, and even death, under the glare of spotlights. A rock upon which the waves of high enthusiasm could expend their energy until they became practised excellence.

Two more would-be daredevils completed the quartet. Both Americans. A man, of about Charlie's age, and his curvacious cousin, to add glamour to the act.

And they practised.

The Knie organisation absorbed them, employed them, but gave them enough free time to work at becoming one more thread in the endless tapestry of circus history.

They learned how to fall; how to hit the net, without dislocating joints or breaking bones. The catcher deliberately mistimed the swings, knowing that they *would* fall; knowing that even the best have 'off' nights and that an unplanned drop onto the net can cripple, unless there is a muscular and nervous reaction, as unconscious—as natural—as the blink of an eye, or the movement of feet, when walking.

The catcher said, 'To hit the net. That, too, is important. The net, proper. Not the apron of the net. The apron is like a badly sprung trampoline. It can even throw you into the audience.'

They worked, they practised and they talked.

The catcher said, 'There will be no deliberate misses. Some acts do this. But not the best acts. Some acts make a deliberate miss, on their difficult tricks. It makes the trick look even more difficult. But what if there is then an accidental miss? Two misses in a row. The act then looks foolish. Unpractised. Unprofessional. There will be no deliberate misses.'

They decided upon a name. 'The Goodwin Troup'.

They pooled their money, and bought new equipment; white, nylon lines and stainless steel bars—spangled tights and flowing, scarlet-lined entrance robes.

And they worked, they practised and they talked.

The catcher said, 'Like the animals, you eat *after* the act. You drink *after* the act. A small thing, but important. Stomach cramp. And you always accept that, on this night, you might fall. They all fall. It is part of the discipline. To fall, occasionally. To know that even the best acts fall. That it is a good week when you do not have at least one fall. That to go a whole month, without a fall, is very exceptional. Up there, you are playing a game with gravity. And, sometimes, gravity must win. Were it otherwise, anybody could be a flyer.'

In little more than a year, they became flyers. Not yet world class, but good enough to perform before an audience.

The Circus Knie took them from menial work, and included them in their programme. Not top billing—animal acts were the Knie speciality, and only the world's best flyers could share top billing with the world's best animal acts ... but 'The Goodwin Troup' had, at least, a place in the programme.

They travelled, they performed, they practised.

They became known and respected. A workmanlike trapeze act. A reliable act, without too much flash and without padding. Cross-overs. One-and-a-halfs. Twos. Eventually, two-and-a-halfs ... but never the magnificent triple. They never quite made the triple ... even in practice.

No matter. Some of the best flying acts in the world never attain the triple.

And the rock was still the catcher.

Each night, he crossed himself before stepping into the ring.

After each performance, he again crossed himself, and murmured, 'Thank God. One less.'

Charlie wondered, and worried a little. 'The Goodwin Troup' was built upon the catcher—*all* flying troups are, in part—and the rock showed signs of crumbling.

Then, one night, it happened ... his nerve went.

He crossed himself but, instead of stepping proudly into the ring, he turned and walked back to the dressing room. He refused to speak. He refused to explain. He simply dressed himself in his street clothes, and left.

A flyer who had become too old for his art. A catcher who chose disgrace, rather than the possibility of injury to his colleagues.

The end of 'The Goodwin Troup'.

'Nice going, Charlie.' I give him the old, sarcastic smile. 'You should learn to whistle.'

The D.I. believes all this 'circus' crap, nods sadly and says, 'Rough luck. How long ago was that?'

'Five years,' says Charlie.

'And, since then?'

'Since then, he's been robbing banks,' I growl.

'No!' Before Charlie can answer his question, the D.I. waves a hand. 'We don't want to know. It might incriminate you.'

'Holy cow!' I breathe.

'Hey, Cameron.' Charlie talks directly at me, for the first time. 'What the hell's with it? You're still the hard nut—okay ... but some people change.'

'Like you?' I sneer.

'It's not impossible.'

'Uhuh ... and some people believe in hobgoblins.'

'Why the hell *not*?'

'Charlie,' I say, in a tired voice, 'we add up to three. Right? And one of us held up a bank, then shot the legs from under a very fancy police officer. And, sure as hell it wasn't *me*. And, for a fact, it wasn't *him*. So that puts you on a very short shortlist, Charlie. Am I getting through?'

'Stick to the circus, Goodwin,' interrupts the D.I. 'It's safer, all round. What else.'

Charlie watches my face, as he says, 'These two clowns. No names, no packdrill. You know 'em ... they're world famous. In the ring, they're a riot. Slapstick. The water routine. Everything. The kids love 'em. Outside the ring, they ignore each other. Hate each other ... they haven't even spoken to each other, for ten years.'

'It's almost unbelievable,' says the D.I.

'It *is* unbelievable,' I grunt. 'Like everything else this bastard says ... unbelievable.'

CHAPTER FOUR

I doze.

The last time I glanced at my watch, it was half-past one, in the small hours.

The fire is banked for the night. The Tilley has been turned low. Outside, the wind has eased considerably. Inside, it is warm and dry, and we have all had a very busy day.

Before I settled down for the night, I had certain things to do. Basic things, but very necessary things ... and some of them I didn't particularly enjoy. The D.I., for example. He's human. He has normal bodily functions ... but he also has two smashed legs. I carried him out into the back, and we were both embarrassed ... but I think he was also grateful. Charlie, for example. Charlie is the original cart-load of monkeys. He doesn't even need a yard ... he'll take a mile if you give him a hair's breadth. And being linked to the bed wasn't safe enough. Not for me. Not all night. So-o, I uncoupled him from the bed and hand-cuffed one of his wrists to the upper leg of one of the chairs. Then, I settled in the other chair, hoisted my feet onto Charlie's wrist-extension and figured that any undue movement on the part of Charles would bring me to my feet, and ready.

I wasn't going to sleep. The hell I was going to sleep, with Charlie in the same room!

By midnight, the D.I. was making muted buzz-saw

noises. Snoring very well-mannered snores ... but, of course, being 'New Scotland Yard'. In between the rasps he mumbled a little, now and then. Words which weren't words. Puppy-dog whimperings, which didn't make sense, until you remembered the legs and the pain he must have sweated his way through. Then, they made sense. Bad sense ... because they could be the first wavelets of delayed shock. And delayed shock can cause problems.

By midnight, Charlie was curled up, foetus-fashion, on the flagstones. He was asleep, but not snoring. Moderately comfortable, with the upper arm of his manacled hand forming a pillow. Not snoring, but inhaling the deep, chest-expanding breaths of untroubled slumber.

Safe?

Charlie Goodwin is *never* 'safe'.

So, I wasn't going to sleep. The hell I was going to sleep, with Charlie in the same room.

The hell I was *not* going to sleep!

I awaken in a hurry, as my stockinged feet hit the stones.

I am upright, and already reaching for the blackjack, as Charlie yells, 'Hold it, Cameron!'

I freeze.

He has me. Anybody else—anybody, but Charlie—and I might have called the bluff. But not Charlie. Charlie isn't bluffing. Charlie will do it ... and with a smile on his face.

He is at the bed. His left hand—the hand with the chair still attached—holds the head of the D.I. rock-steady. It grips the far side of the neck, with the thumb thrusting the jaw bone high and stretching the throat. In his right hand is the pocket knife. *My* pocket knife ... the one I slung away, in disgust, after I'd performed my Emergency

Ward Ten act. The spike is closed. The blade is open, and the blade is already biting into the throat of the D.I. It is already into the side of the throat—the left side of the throat, where it can rip in, behind the windpipe—and, in the glow from the lowered Tilley, I estimate that a quarter of an inch of steel is already home and tasting blood.

The blood is dark, and shiny in the glow from the Tilley and the amber illumination from the fire.

The D.I. isn't snoring any more. He is wide-eyed and motionless.

I stay frozen, but say, 'Put it down, Charlie. You can't run for it . . . not with that stuff, outside.'

'Don't try anything, Cameron.'

'Drop the knife, Charlie. Go back to sleep.'

'I'll slit him open, Cameron. Don't ever think I won't.'

The D.I. chokes, 'Don't do it, Cameron. *Anything*. He daren't go through with it. It would be murder.'

That takes some saying; with a bastard like Charlie, and a knife at your throat, that brand of remark makes you man-sized . . . even if you are from the wrong end of the country.

I pass the New Scotland Yard berk a quick smile of pity, and say, 'That thought should be very comforting, while you're on your way to hell, sonny.'

'You know me better, Cameron,' warns Charlie, softly.

'I know you better.' I nod, sadly. 'I know you better than any other man alive.' I play for time, and add, 'When did you get hold of the knife, Charlie? When I took Laughing Boy for a piss?'

His eyes answer me, and tell me I've guessed right.

I say, 'I'm going to turn the lamp up, Charlie,' and I am still playing for time.

'Don't do anything stupid, Cameron.'

'Would I?'

'Like throwing the lamp.'

'Would I do such a stupid thing?'

'His throat comes out, if you do.'

'Of course, Charlie. Did I ever disbelieve you?'

The D.I. whispers, 'He's bluffing, Cameron. He's *bluffing.*'

'No.' I shake my head, slowly. 'This is something you don't understand, sonny. This is a league you haven't even heard of.'

Charlie moves his head in agreement. This is, indeed, something the gold-plated 'Met' will never get alongside. This is wild country. Jungle country. The domain of predators ... and God help the vegetarians.

I take a couple of steps, to within reach of the lamp. Slow steps. Careful steps. Then, as I reach out and turn up the lamp. Slowly. Carefully. As if I am unravelling a spider's web ... as slowly and carefully as *that.*

Charlie watches me, and the blade is ready to do its killing work before the base of the lamp could even leave the table.

With light, we can see better.

Charlie's unclosed eye verifies what I already know. That this is no come-on; that the life of the D.I. is in hock, pending my good behaviour; that he is living on a strict 'pay-and-promise' basis, unless I breathe at whichever tempo Charlie decrees.

Could be the D.I. doesn't know this.

Could be the extra pain has turned his thinking equipment into scrambled egg.

And he *is* in extra pain. Discounting the blade—which, itself, is no soothing balm—Charlie's dive onto the bed, to get into a position to make his play, has corkscrewed the legs and the splints to hell and beyond. Even under the cover of the blankets, this can be seen.

The teeth are clenched. The colour of the face is the colour of yellowing candle-wax. And the forehead and upper lip carry droplets of sweat, as big as boiled sago.

The kid can take it ... but, how much more, and for how much longer, is anybody's guess.

I take my hands away from the lamp, and say, 'Your move, Charlie.'

'Get these cuffs off.'

'Don't,' croaks the D.I. 'Don't do it, Cameron.'

Nobody is listening to the D.I.

I smile, and say, 'You're living dangerously, Charlie.

'Do it.'

'It means me coming within belting distance.'

'Go ahead, and belt.' The good eye watches me.

'And?'

'There's a shovel in the back. You can use it to bury this creep.'

'I believe you, Charlie,' I sigh.

'Don't ever *not*.'

I shrug, and move closer. The left hand tightens on the neck of the D.I. The thumb forces the chin higher. The right hand grips the knife, and the right arm tenses, ready to drive the blade home.

I murmur, 'Relax, Charlie. You hold the aces.'

He says, 'First, the chair.'

'Sure.'

'As if you're walking on eggs, Cameron.'

'Slowly, and gently,' I agree. 'I need the key. It's in my pocket.'

'Slowly, and gently,' he warns.

He knows I'm going to try something. He knows I *have*

59

to. What he *doesn't* know is what, and when. That is the only slice of surprise I have left and, when I have used that up, I have nothing. Nothing!

I ease the key from my pocket. Hold it in my thumb and forefinger, for him to see. For him to watch ... and worry about.

'Ready?' I ask, teasingly.

He repeats, 'Slowly, and gently,' and the tone carries subtle shades of anxiety.

'But, of course,' I mock.

It is a very nervy situation. For Charlie, and for the D.I. But not for me. *My* throat doesn't have a blade within ripping distance. *My* hand isn't anchored to a kitchen chair.

I am sending Charlie silent messages, and he is receiving them, loud and clear. Supposing I couldn't care less about the D.I.? ... which, in fact, I couldn't. Supposing I don't give a damn whether he has a throat, or not? ... which, in fact, I don't.

Charlie is a dead duck. And he knows it. I can have him—I can break his stupid neck—and my full, and absolute, justification will be a dead detective inspector.

All it needs is a little ruthlessness, on my part ... and I have a reputation.

I can see it in Charlie's eye. The realisation. That all these aces he figured he was holding aren't aces any more. They are all suddenly deuces ... and the game we are playing makes Blind Brag kindergarten stuff.

I chuckle, quietly, and he knows I have him—and he knows *I* know he knows ... and it shreds his nerves to hell.

Charlie, you're a mug. For the first time in your rotten life, you're a mug. You've under-estimated, Charlie. You don't know what *real* hatred is. What it can do. How far it can drive. But you're learning ... that you could kill the whole damn world, and it wouldn't matter, because the price would be acceptable. I'd willingly pay the price for the pleasure of sending you back to whatever bastard made you.

You're dead, Charlie ... *you are dead!*

I whisper, 'Charlie's dead, sweetheart. I'm sorry, but there's no easy way of saying it. Charlie's dead.'

'No. He's not dead. You're wrong, he's not dead.'

I hold her tight, stroke her hair and look across her shoulder, at the medic. I need guidance. I need to know what to say—what to do—but the medic is as helpless as I am. He is a good medic. He knows his profession. But, like me, he is worried sick at her refusal to accept the truth.

He begins, 'Mrs. Cameron. I'm sorry, but...'

'I don't want to know.' She turns, in my arms, and spits her fury at him. 'You, and your kind. You're liars. You tell lies, about my child. My husband might believe you ... but I don't.'

'He's dead, honey,' I breathe. 'I wish to hell it wasn't so, but he's...'

'HE IS NOT DEAD!'

She screams the words, and the medic backs off a pace, as if he is afraid she might fly at his throat.

'Honey,' I soothe. 'Honey, take it easy. Nobody's going to hurt you ... not while I'm around.'

'All right.' She turns onto me, and snarls, 'Tell them he's not dead. Tell them they're liars. That Charlie isn't dead.'

Somewhere in the universe there is an answer. But I don't have it.

The medic has an answer ... of a sort.

He motions to the nurse, standing nearby, and says, 'Take Mrs. Cameron to lie down, staff. Make her comfortable. I'll be along in a few minutes.'

She looks up at my face, as the nurse touches her elbow and, already, her eyes house the lifeless gaze of a crazy woman.

I murmur, 'Go with her, honey,' ... and I feel like Judas.

When they are out of earshot, and out of sight, the medic shakes his head and sighs, 'She's taken it badly.'

I nod. I want to ask a question ... but daren't.

'Badly,' he repeats, like an unhappy echo.

'How badly?' I ask ... and that, in essence, is my question.

The medic says, 'I think we should sit down, Mr. Cameron.'

I follow him along the corridor, and into a ward sister's office. He waves me into a chair and offers me a cigarette. When we are both smoking, he answers my question, as dogmatically as his profession will allow.

He says, 'You're a police constable, I understand?'

'P.C. Cameron.'

'Not a young man. By that, I mean not a grass green recruit.'

'I've lived a few years. Seen a few things.'

'Your child?' he asks. 'Your son? What conclusions had you reached?'

'E.S.N.,' I say, flatly.

'Educationally sub-normal.'

'But more than that. Worse than that ... that was my opinion.'

'Quite.' He chooses his words with infinite care. 'He

*would never have been quite normal ... short of a miracle.
Not mongoloid, of course, but ...'*

'But, almost.' I end the sentence for him.

He draws on his cigarette, and says, 'Three years old.'

'Would have been, next month.'

'And he couldn't yet speak. Couldn't yet say "mummy"
or "daddy".'

'He wasn't even house-trained,' I growl.

He looks sad, and says, 'I'm sorry, Mr. Cameron. I'm
sorry.'

'She wouldn't accept it. That he was—er ... imperfect.
They sometimes won't. Mothers, I mean. Accept that their
kids are ...'

There is a silence, then the medic says, 'Any more than
she'll now accept that he's dead.'

'Funny,' I muse.

'What?'

'She doesn't blame me.'

'How can she? As far as she's concerned, he's not yet
dead. To acknowledge the one would require the acceptance of the other.'

'Neat.'

'Logical.' He smiles a sad, and weary, smile. 'The sick
mind is capable of its own sick logic, Mr. Cameron.'

'This—er—"sickness"?' I ask, softly. 'How long?'

'It could be a long time,' he fences.

'How long?'

He hesitates, then says, 'It could be for the rest of her
life.'

'Could be? ... or will be?'

'I'm sorry. Quite probably will be.'

'The chair,' whispers Charlie. 'Start by uncuffing the chair.'

'Sure.'

'And, Cameron, don't try anything. Don't even look as if you *might* try something.'

'As if I would, Charlie. As if I would.'

But, he knows damn well I'm going to.

I unlock the chair from his wrist. Ve-ery slowly; as slowly, and as smoothly, as any trick movie showing the movement of birds in flight. I have made him edgy. My next move is to relax him a little; to take some of the edginess away, and give him a feeling of safety. To play yo-yo with his nerves. To make him unsure.

I take the key from the lock of the cuff, then lift the chair from the bed and place it on the flagstones of the floor.

There is a moment—a split second—when he thinks I am going to smack him with the chair. The perfect set-up. The obvious move ... therefore, the move he is waiting for and the move I won't make.

The D.I. expected it. I can spot it in his eyes—the little-boy-disappointed look—as I place the chair carefully on the flagstones. He expected me to swing the chair—as Charlie expected me to swing the chair ... a stupid, 'New Scotland Yard' gamble, which would have had every card in the deck marked.

I place the chair, very carefully, then, in a mock-innocent voice, ask, 'You want the other bracelet off, Charlie?'

'Don't arse around, Cameron. Unlock it.'

It's there. The slight tremor in his voice. The can't-be-kept-down uncertainty, which insists that this could be the craziest thing he has done in his whole, rotten life.

Charlie, boy ... how right you are.

The banked fire shifts, and the tiny noise makes him jerk and tighten the grip on the knife. That's how jumpy he is. That's how *scared* he is ... but inside. Outside, he makes believe he has the situation under control; that he is the boss, and that he still holds the aces. But, inside, his guts have turned to whey.

And that's how I need him. Ripped down the middle, by his own fluttering nerves.

I lean over the bed, and reach towards the hand holding the knife; towards the wrist with the handcuffs still attached. I touch the metal of the cuffs ... then I move!

I smash the blade of my palm into the bend of his right elbow and, at the same time, swing my right leg to scythe him behind the knees. The knife jerks from the throat, fractionally before he starts to totter and has to pull his left hand away from the D.I., in order to save his balance.

I pivot on my left foot, and aim a roundhouse swing at his face with my left fist. It is all wrong—left doesn't go with left, in brawling—and I am being over-ambitious. I miss, completely, and give him time to duck from under and get ready to fight.

And another thing. The chop into the flesh of the right arm. Once upon a time, Charlie had slabs of meat there. Not fat, but heavy meat. Not any more. What is there now is all muscle. Hard muscle; hard enough to let me know I've collided with it with the side of my hand.

I do a little quick re-assessment. I can take him—I can still take him ... but it isn't going to be the pushover I expected.

He is bent-legged and balanced. The puny blade making silly circles in the air, as he waits for the rush.

I watch him, feint with the left then, as his eye follows the feint, reach for the chair with my right. He wants to play rough-house? ... That's fine by me.

He spots the chair, sways, then dives for the twelve-bore, which is leaning against the wall, behind him. The chair follows him, and smacks him at the nape of the neck, as his hand closes around the barrel of the shotgun. He straightens, turns and comes at me, flailing the shotgun like a woodman's axe.

I dance out of his reach, laugh at him, and taunt, 'You're almost a man, Charlie. You've learned how to fight.'

I feel the edge of the bed, against the back of my legs, and know I've backed as far as I'm able to back. Charlie knows it, too. He stops flailing the shotgun, and makes his first mistake. He raises it, for a straight-down smash.

He has a blind side. His left side is his blind side, and I wait for the shotgun to start its downward slash, then duck to my right, close in and hammer a hard-fisted punch into the mangled half of his face.

It hurts. It makes him gasp and, as he swings to his left, I move with him, scoop up the chair, en route, and hurt him some more with the edge of the chair against the left side of his skull.

He drops the gun, grunts some naughty words, and almost goes down.

I don't want him to go down ... not yet.

He is where I want him—where I've wanted him, for half a lifetime—and I have some bile to work out of my system, before I allow him to go down.

I toss the chair aside, and move in with my fists.

This, I have dreamed about. A hundred nights, I have dreamed this dream; that Charlie Goodwin is within smacking distance, and that I am free to cut loose on him, as hard and as often as he can take it. This is a dream, come true.

Christ knows how many times I hit him. I don't bother to count. As often as possible ... that's all. Nothing scien-

tific; just simple, swinging lefts and rights—lefts and rights
—which bomb his face and head, and explode all fight
out of him.

He sprawls on the bed—across the legs of the D.I.—
and the D.I. lets out a high-pitched sob of agony.

I close my fingers around a handful of shirt, yank him
from the bed, slam him against a wall and hold him there,
while I paste blue crap out of that lousy, treacherous face.

'Cameron!'

For him ... for her ... for me ...

'*Cameron!*'

... for the tears ... for the heartache ... for the misery ...

'*CAMERON!*'

It reaches me. That somebody is yelling my name. That
I am beating the life out of this bastard ... and that somebody is anxious that I should stop, before I completely
finish him.

I lower my muscle-weary right arm to my side, and
unclench the fingers of my left hand. Charlie drops, rag-
doll limp, into the angle of the wall and the floor. I turn,
slowly, and look towards the bed.

'For Christ's sake, Cameron,' gasps the D.I. 'Have you
gone completely crazy?'

I try to nod, but haven't the energy for it. Instead, I
gulp in air and stare at this M.P.D. jack who has visited
all this anguish upon me.

He is worth a second glance.

I swear, I have seen healthier things stretched out on a
morgue slab. His eye-sockets are like dark caves, with the
eyes, fires smouldering deep inside those caves. His hair is
plastered to his skull with sweat; sweat runs, in streams,
down the parchment-white of his face and dilutes the still-
running blood from the knife-cut at the side of his throat.

He has lips—every mouth has lips—but they have no
colour, other than the colour of the rest of his face. When
he speaks, his voice is harsh and weak ... like a death
rattle.

I walk to the chair—the chair I fell asleep on—and my
legs are a little unsteady. My knees tremble a little. I sit
on the chair, and I realise I am very happy to sit on the
chair.

The D.I. croaks, 'Your mouth.'

'Eh?'

'Didn't you know?'

I touch my lips, and my fingers come away scarlet. I
explore, with my tongue, and find two tender gaps where
there should be teeth. Charlie, too, has slugged ... but I
don't remember. You have my solemn oath. I don't
remember him hitting me once.

And, suddenly, I get the shakes.

I rest my forearms on my knees, drop my chin onto
my chest and oscillate like a blancmange in an earthquake. I can't do a thing about it. I clench my fists and
hold my arms tight against my sides, but it doesn't mean
a damn. The staggers continue for all of five, long minutes.

The D.I. rasps, 'Cameron. Cameron ... are you all right?'

I can't even answer.

I try to nod ... but all I do is splash blood from my
mouth down the front of my shirt.

Gradually, the shakes leave me.

I take a few deep breaths, raise my chin, shake my head
to clear the last of the spooks from my brain, then say,
'Sure. I'm fine. I never felt better.'

Which (I admit) is some slight exaggeration.

The room has turned cold ... that, or my personal
thermostat isn't functioning as well as it should. I take

a log, break up the crust of the banked fire, then throw the log, along with three other logs, into the stirred-up blaze. The wood spits and cracks, then blackens as the flames take hold.

I check that Charlie is still in Outer Space, before I move to the bed.

I look down at the D.I., and say, 'Jesus!'

The feverish eyes look back a question.

I say, 'Sonny, why the hell didn't you stay down South? Why the hell come and mix it with grown men?'

'You think I'm some brand of poofter?' he challenges.

'No. I think you can take your fair share of stick, sonny. Maybe more than your fair share. But, up here, that isn't good enough.'

'It's necessary to dish it out. Is that it?'

'It helps,' I agree.

He tries a smile, but it doesn't quite fit, as he mutters, 'From what I've seen, you can dish it out for both of us.'

'Uhuh.'

'What's it like, outside?'

'The—er...' I remember, with something of a shock, that what happens beyond these walls is also important. Something which has slipped my memory. I say, 'The wind's dropped. That's one blessing. Maybe the snow's stopped, too ... I haven't looked, recently.'

'That could mean a chopper, by morning.'

I grunt some sort of reply. Who the hell am I to pull straws from his hand? In his shoes I, too, might indulge in a few doses of wishful thinking.

He says, 'What time is it?'

I glance at my watch, and tell him, 'After two. Almost half-past.'

'They say...' he begins, ruefully, then stops.

'What?'

'Three o'clock—four o'clock ... the time when life ebbs.'

'Hey, come on,' I protest. 'You're a hero, sonny. You have medals to collect.'

'Some bloody hero!'

'Five gets you ten, you'll end up at Buck House.'

'Knock it off, Cameron.'

'The Met?' I kid him. 'The one-and-only New Scotland Yard? Sonny, they won't be able to gazette you fast enough.'

This time, the smile makes it ... just.

I grin back at him, and say, 'But, first, the clean-up. Then, you need a little lead injecting into your pencil.'

He murmurs, 'You're the boss, Cameron ... and, thanks.'

Big deal, wouldn't you say? A high point in the life of any provincial, pavement-bashing jack? When a New Scotland Yard detective inspector (no less) steps into second place; when the 'sir' routine gets reversed, and the humble *really* inherit the earth.

We-ell—maybe not too humble ... I wouldn't argue.

But a nice feeling, nevertheless.

I move into action once more. I pick up the handcuff key, from where I dropped it, alongside the bed. I grab the still-slumbering Charlie by the back of his collar, drag him into the scullery and link him to the wrought-iron-pump-pipe, again. Then I sluice my face, swill the blood from my mouth, run cold water over the split skin of my knuckles and, finally, dry myself.

Then, back to the main room, with pail, water and cloths.

The D.I. repeats his teeth-gritting, while I encore my bone-setting trick. It isn't nice. Nor is it very satisfactory. The human frame can take only so much, and flesh can

70

be mangled only so far. At a rough estimate, we're within touching distance of the limits ... and I wouldn't be too surprised to learn that we've passed the limits.

But what else?

Okay—it is like using Polycell as a substitute for re-inforced concrete ... but what the hell else? Could be he needs a blood transfusion. I'm not arguing—I'm merely stating a rather nasty fact ... that he isn't going to *get* a blood transfusion. Not yet. Not today, and maybe not tomorrow. Within a week ... if he's lucky. If he can keep breathing for another week.

And, if he can't ... what the hell *else*?

I wash the sweat and blood from his face and neck, then work the primus and make some tea. Hot, sweet tea, heavily laced with whisky. We both need it. And I care not that some First Aid whizz-kid, sitting in some upholstered office, has decreed that alcohol is not the best antidote for shock; that getting quietly gassed is no solu-tion to the problem of physical injury. We aren't in an upholstered office, and booze is the only analgesic avail-able. So-o ... booze it is, because booze it has to be.

He sips the tea, eyes me quizzically, and says, 'You're a strange man, Cameron.'

'Strange?'

'Hard ... but soft-centred.'

'Mind your teeth, sonny,' I growl. 'That soft-centre you're on about. It hides steel ball-bearings.'

'I think not.'

'Ask him.' I jerk my head towards the door, leading to the scullery. 'He had thoughts, along the same lines. Now, he *knows*.'

He observes the obvious, and says, 'You hate him?'

'In passing,' I agree.

'Why?'

'He's the enemy. *My* enemy.'

'Because you're a police officer?'

'I'm no lay preacher,' I say. 'All that "love thy enemy" stuff leaves me cold.'

'And yet, you're a good copper.'

'Don't look for a unanimous vote on that proposal. Men, of some rank, would at least abstain.'

'But sour,' he adds.

'Sour. Hard. Bitter.' I shrug. 'They're words, friend. They can be used to describe lemons, or diamonds. And anything between.'

'And hatred?'

I chew it around in my mind, for a moment, then say, 'It proves concern. That you're aware. Okay ... that you even have feeling for. I'm not arguing that it's an aspect of love. Don't get me wrong. Maybe love, turned inside-out ... no more than that. But it proves concern. That he—she, it—gets well up your nostrils. You can't hate, without noticing whatever it is you hate. To that extent, it isn't an abstract thing. It has to have something to latch onto ... and a reason.'

'And the reason?' His voice is still hoarse—still weak —and the whisky is giving it the hint of a slur, but it carries the curiosity of the snooper. The copper, if you like. He says, 'Specifically, *your* reason? For hating Goodwin?'

'I don't hate Charlie,' I lie. 'We're one-time buddies ... remember? It's just that I know him. Know him for the roughneck he is. I know him well enough to mistrust him. Not to give him an edge. That's why I'm sitting on this chair, sonny. Why you're on that bed, and why Charlie's on the floor in the scullery.'

CHAPTER FIVE

The small hours. That's what they call them. The be-witching hours. The silent hours. The mystic hours.

All those names, and a score of other names, all thought up by jerks for whom that particular o'clock is a great novelty. Romantics. Love-lorn loons, who don't have to push pavements through those hours; who spend them, either philosophising about the riddle of romance or (on a more practical basis) holding some female to their manly chests, while they work up the energy for the next screw.

Now (as the saying goes) ask a policeman.

He'll tell you; that those hours may be 'small', but they're also the longest hours on the whole clock face; that they may be 'silent', but their silence is the silence of a rifled tomb; that the only 'bewitching' thing about them can be traced to the mild trick of hallucination played by eyes which are being forced to watch, when they should be closed, and the only 'romance' abroad is the romance of the alley-cats going about their fornicatory business.

That wedge of time should have been outlawed, light-years back. It belongs to the Dark Ages. It has aching muscles attached. And a willingness to give in. It slips life, itself, onto a very loose rein, and the old boy with the scythe across his thin shoulder strolls around, and touches far too many people with his bony fingers.

If you have a tendency to believe in bogey-men, that is

the time of night when suspicion steps across the line dividing doubt from certainty.

Take the 'small hours'.

For me, you can have them, as a gift.

By four o'clock, the D.I. was asleep; asleep, or unconscious ... I wouldn't take bets which. On his back, with his eyes closed and his mouth open, making soft moaning noises, with gurglings attached, from deep in his stretched throat.

A detective inspector ... at *his* age!

What the hell does the Met look for in a man? What makes this one so much different? What makes him so much better than the leather-stampers who stroll alongside the protest marchers?

He has guts—okay, he has guts ... he has absorbed more punishment than any man of his age should be expected to absorb and, to his credit, he hasn't screamed too loudly. That makes him a tough nut, or a mug. You take your pick. Me? ... I figure him both. What happened to his legs was his own fault; when you're calling on men who have the habit of waving guns around in public, you don't send visiting cards; you don't announce yourself, until you've arrived; you don't knock on doors and request an audience. To that extent, he is a mug and, to that extent, he can be blamed for this whole aggravated lash-up.

Ah, well—maybe that is the 'New Scotland Yard' way ... if so, the sooner they form a death-and-divide club, the better.

He is a mug in other ways, too.

He tries to be a cop and the gentleman, and the two don't mix. He acts like he is playing cricket—like there is an umpire around, to make sure the rules are not broken ... and that the opposing team will stick strictly to those rules. Sweet Jesus! One day he will learn. That the opposing team will happily kick the umpire in the crotch, in order to divert attention, while they beat every lawman in sight over the head with every bat they can get their hands on.

One day he will learn ... and maybe today has been that day.

And maybe he will live to take advantage of that lesson.

Nevertheless, he has guts.

That they are shot-shit-and-shell guts makes them no less gutsy. That they carry the brand-mark of 'stiff-upper-lip' makes them no less real. I have known reputed tough guys squeal like stuck pigs ... and at a lot less.

But today is something he will describe to his grand-children. Assuming he lives long enough to have grand-children.

He will tell them ... about the day he was caught in the cross-fire, between Ray Cameron and Charlie Goodwin.

Meanwhile, he sleeps.

Or is, perhaps, unconscious.

At four-fifteen (thereabouts), I heard noises from the scullery.

I hoisted myself from the chair, took the blackjack from the shelf, above the fireplace, and cat-footed in to investigate.

Charlie was busy bringing himself back to near-normality. He'd wriggled the cuffs up the water-pipe, until one hand was within reaching distance of the pump handle ... just. He was working the handle and, as the water gushed, he was ducking his head and shoulders under the flow; catching as much as he could, before it weakened to a trickle, and he had to pump the handle again.

I watched him for a few moments, before he spotted me.

He stopped his contortions, and stared at me from behind his mangled features.

His puffed lips formed words, and he sneered, 'Worried?'

'Cautious ... no more than that, Charlie.'

He said, 'I'm still alive. That should worry you.'

'You'll live,' I assured him. 'Since topping went out of vogue, bastards like you will live forever.'

He growled, 'I wouldn't have what's living inside you for a million, Cameron.'

'I believe you ... and without diagrams.'

'Whatever it is, it's screwed you up, crazy.'

'Whatever's inside, you put there,' I said, flatly.

He didn't understand. He shook his head, in puzzlement, and water droplets cascaded from his hair, and from his soaked face, and sprinkled the stones around his feet.

I stepped into the scullery, tossed the rough towel to within his reach, and said, 'Wipe the blood off, Charlie. As much of it as you're able ... which is a hell of a long way from *all.*'

I left him, and he still didn't understand.

Or, maybe he was playing dumb. Acting an innocence which isn't there.

Who knows?

Charlie? ... He is something of a museum-piece. Always was. Peter Pan, in person; the fink who never grew up; the lousy bastard who never acknowledged the responsibilities of adulthood.

He *should* know. My aching back, he *should* know!

But it is possible. Just possible. If all that crap about circuses, and flyers, was not crap, after all—if, for the more important years, he's been tooling around the Continent, playing swings under big-tops ... then, it is just possible.

'Ignorance is no excuse' ... that's what the law says. And, although I have been known to thumb a nose at the law, occasionally, this time I take its point. It makes for an easier conscience. I have wasted a short lifetime, if there is ignorance, unless 'ignorance is no excuse'.

Ignorance, my arse!

I don't give one single damn whether he knows, or whether he doesn't know. He *should* know. He should have made it his business to know. Every other bastard knew—every other bastard still knows ... so why not him?

Charlie—you're *Charlie* ... that's all that matters.

She says, 'This is Charlie,' and those three words are the first words she has spoken, since I arrived.

For more than an hour I have sat opposite her. I have watched the emptiness of her expression—the blankness of her eyes—and I have tried to batter a way through, with my feelings for her.

'Honey, I love you. This is Ray. Ray, telling you he loves you.'

'Honey, it doesn't matter. Nobody's going to hurt you. Nobody! I'll not let anybody hurt you ... believe me.'

It is like talking to a brick. A brick—not a cabbage ... let nobody who values their teeth call her a cabbage.

The duty witch doctor wanders up, joins us and smiles a welcome.

He croons, 'Are you pleased to see your husband again, Mrs. Cameron?'

Bricks can't hear, and bricks can't answer ... so he doesn't get a reaction.

He beams at me, and says, 'Well, what do you think, Mr. Cameron?'

I should have my tongue ripped out at the roots for saying it, but it's the truth ... so, what the hell? It needs saying. We have all hedged far too many bets, and for far too long. We have wanted things too badly and, by wanting them too badly, we've blinkered ourselves into seeing only what we've hoped to see.

I tear the blinkers aside, and say, 'She's no better.'

'Oh, I wouldn't go as far as ...'

'In fact, she's worse.'

'I'm sorry, Mr. Cameron. You're in no position to pass ...'

'I come here, twice a week. Every week. For months, now. For years. Don't throw academic dust in my eyes, doc. I can see for myself.'

'It's a slow process, Mr. Cameron. You were warned.'

'I know. And that it might not work.'

'We can't be sure,' he sighs.

'I'm sure.'

He looks sad. I don't doubt but that he is a compassionate man. I wish he was also a truthful man.

Some sort of half-life flickers behind her eyes, and she repeats, 'This is Charlie.'

She holds the tattered teddy bear out, in a gesture of crazy introduction.

I touch the teddy bear's head, and murmur, 'Okay, sweetheart. I know ... that's Charlie. I like him, a lot. And —sweetheart—you don't know what I'm saying, but that doesn't make it any less true. I love you, honey. As God's my judge, I love you.'

I stand up, and walk out of the ward.

But I don't weep—I am not one of the weepers of the

world ... so what the hell are my cheeks doing wet?

I haven't seen her, since.

Emotion can take just so much. It varies—some people can hold more emotional pain than others—but everybody has a top-up point. Nobody can absorb it, forever; can come up for more until Doom cracks; can smile at, and talk to, and love ... a *brick*.

That day, I spilled over ... and I haven't seen her since.

Which (I know) makes me a louse, but—okay—I have learned to live with a louse.

But I am not quite the biggest louse walking the earth.

The top spot belongs to Charlie.

CHAPTER SIX

Up in these parts, there is no bay—nor can you view China
—therefore, very much unlike the song, dawn does *not*
'come up like thunder'. In these parts, it creeps in, like
a sneak-thief; very gradually, the windows look a little
less like pitch mirrors; very slowly, the Tilley seems to
grow dimmer; then, almost with a shock, you realise that
the light from outside has taken over from the light which
the lamp has given you all night, and you can stop burn-
ing paraffin.

I turn out the lamp, and go into the scullery.

Charlie is asleep. How the hell he sleeps, with his shoulder blades wedged between the wall and the water pipe—
with his shirt still damp with near-freezing water, and with
one wrist linked to the iron of the pipe—is his own personal parlour trick. I couldn't do it. But, come to that, I
couldn't be a high-trapeze flyer—supposing he ever *was*
... so, what the hell does that prove?

I open the shot-blasted door, and paddle out into the
snow for the first piss of the day.

And I know the weather is still playing puss-in-the-corner
with us.

The wind has dropped, the snow has stopped, and
centre-stage has now been taken over by mist.

This mist, too, is a 'Tops Speciality'.

Somewhere—in the Mountain Rescue Team office, maybe

—they have figures showing how many people this damn stuff has robbed of life. The list is three figures thick ... maybe more. Nor were they all mugs. The mist of these parts scares the pants off the experts. Grey ... like walking through a cloud. Never-ending, and never still. Not of one consistency, and not of one thickness. It moves, like a living thing; it opens and closes ... one second you can see a few yards ahead, the next second you can't even see your feet.

I zip up my fly, return to the scullery and close the door on this shifting opaqueness.

Charlie is back from Nod.

'How's the weather?' he asks, and it comes out a mumble, from his smashed mouth and swollen lips.

'Where you're going, it never rains,' I crack.

He stays deadpan. To move those facial muscles, more than necessary, would bring on the pain.

I take a long breath, then say, 'The youth's in a bad way.'

'How bad?'

'He's been holding low-voiced arguments with himself, all night.'

'Wet dreams, maybe. Maybe he was shafting Monroe.'

'Don't get clever, Charlie,' I warn. 'You're nicely placed ... I could land my boot in your face, real easy.'

'Sure. And would.'

'Don't ever kid yourself otherwise.'

'So?' he mumbles. 'The big cop talks in his sleep. Who doesn't?'

'He's in bad pain.'

'*I'm* in bad pain.'

'I believe you, Charlie. But, you don't count.'

.'Look, what the hell ...'

I snarl, 'Shove it, Charlie. I'm going to check. You and me could be taking a walk.'

'You must be out of your ...'

'Shove it, Charlie!'

I return to the main room, and go to the cupboard. The inner man needs sustenance, and with as little useless packing as possible. I am told—indeed, hairy-armed 'survival experts' tend to start every conversation with this snippet of useless information—that the human body can tick over for a fortnight (maybe even longer) without food. All it needs is water, warmth and rest. Which is okay, if you're so damn bored with life that floating around in a heated swimming pool is your idea of kicks ... but normal people need nosh.

There is plenty of nosh in the cupboard, thank God. Tins of baked beans. Packs of bacon. Dried egg powder ... and it's a long time since I saw *that*. Beef cubes. Packet soup and tinned soup. Powdered milk and tinned milk. Instant coffee and packets of tea. Sugar. Even a jar of home-made chutney. Everything!

The sheep-chasers around these parts know all there is to know about making up a good store.

There are also a few things I haven't noticed before.

A cardboard box, with a cross painted in red along its top. A home-made First Aid collection. Bandages, sticking-plaster, lint, cotton-wool. Iodine and aspirins. And a tiny tin of ready-to-use tubes of morphine—like the tubes of paint they sell to artists—complete with needled tops ... the sort of pain-numbing gadget the air-crew boys once humped around when they figured the flack barrage might get a little too close for comfort.

And there is also a half-empty box of twelve-bore cartridges ... and, at a guess, this is something Charlie added to this little cache.

On the top shelf, there are tin plates, tin mugs, knives, forks and spoons, and a frying pan.

We're in clover.

Fifteen minutes later, I have a real 'cowboy's breakfast' on the make; scrambled eggs, bacon and beans, with hot coffee to follow.

I go back into the scullery and deliver unto Charlie a simple and/or ultimatum.

I say, 'Smell it?'

He nods, and there is the eagerness of hunger in that single, simple movement.

'You like?' I ask.

'Yeah. Who wouldn't?'

I swing the blackjack, pointedly, and say, 'Behave yourself ... and eat. Try any personal conjuring tricks ... and *you'll* be the one to disappear. Savvy?'

'A truce?' he offers.

'Not forever, Charlie. Don't get me wrong.'

'Name it.'

'One-handed ... and until you've stuffed your guts. After that, I'm open to suggestions.'

'Fine. I'll eat. Then, we'll talk.'

'Don't bust a gut, Charlie,' I warn, in a growling tone. 'You're just shoving your mouth from behind the eight-ball. That's all. The rest of you stays out of play.'

'Would I chance anything? With *you*?'

'You,' I assure him, 'would take on Old Nick himself, at strip-poker ... just for the joy of seeing him without horns and tail.'

And yet, he has behaved himself. Immaculately.

Linked to the bed, he has thawed himself, in front of the fire, and shovelled food into the hole in his battered face, with all the single-mindedness of a starving man. He has even said, 'Thanks' a couple of times and, once, when he accidentally jerked the bed, he looked up at the D.I. and said, 'Sorry.'

The D.I., too, has eaten.

I *ordered* him to eat. Get that? Detective Constable Cameron slapped a cold-voiced instruction into the teeth of a New Scotland Yard detective inspector ... and didn't get the big argument he expected.

Could be we're all wrong, after all. Could be the world *is* square.

And now comes the big moment.

I pass the cigarettes round and, when everybody is busy ruining their lungs, I say, 'We're leaving you, sonny.'

The D.I. blinks half-conscious incomprehension.

Charlie says, 'What's all the "we" talk, Cameron?'

'Close the zip, Charlie,' I snap. 'You don't even merit a postal vote.'

'I'm sorry, I don't ...' begins the D.I.

'That leg.' I try to get it across to him; try to pierce the clouds which I know are fogging his brain. '*Both* those legs. They need seeing to.'

'They're bad. I'm not disputing that. They're bad, but...'

'For Christ's sake!' I explode. 'Don't be more dumb than God made you, sonny. We could wait here, till you're worm meat. You've lost blood. I don't know how much ... but enough to worry me. The bone in that leg—maybe both legs ... I'm damned if I *know*. I'm no expert. I've done my best, but *my* best is a hell of a long way from good enough. Somebody, somewhere, is expecting me to deliver you back, in one piece. That's it, sonny. That's it, and all there is about it. You're staying here. We're moving out—back to civilisation, to contact help.'

'There goes that "we" again,' murmurs Charlie.

'You, too, Charlie,' I say, harshly. 'You're the reason for all this grief. If you have dreams of toasting your toes in front of this fire, while everybody else is screwing their balls off, finding a way out, you've been reading too many Noddy books.'

'I don't see what the hell...'

'Shurrup, Charlie. Be happy I haven't decided to blow your guts out ... that's the only sure way of making sure you behave yourself.'

'Oh!'

'So, be happy, Charlie ... eh?'

He doesn't look happy. But he appreciates the argument, and he has sense enough to know I'm not bluffing.

I unpack one of the tubes of morphine, take the sheath from the needle and move to the bed.

I say, 'I'll try not to be too clumsy, kid. It'll ease the pain. Maybe give you a little shut-eye, till we get back.'

I bare the left arm, and move the needle towards the skin.

Charlie says, 'Don't mind me, Cameron.'

'Eh?'

'You want to kill him, go right ahead.'

I straighten, and say, 'Are you trying to tell me something, Charlie?'

'Two things. That you're going to squirt air into his blood stream ... which, in case you don't know it, cancels our walk in the snow. He'll be stiffening, before we reach the door. And, even if you miss out on that, just under the skin won't do much good. It has to be in a vein.'

'Doctor Goodwin, I presume?' I sneer.

'I've used them,' he says, quietly.

I hesitate, then say, 'Okay. Show me. The right way ... and no clown-dog antics.'

'*He* doesn't hate me,' he says, bitterly.

'No,' I agree. 'And *he* isn't the one who's going to kick your head clear of your shoulders, given only the whisker of an excuse.'

He holds out his unmanacled hand, and sighs, 'The needle, Cameron. And live dangerously ... I need all ten fingers.'

'Trust him,' says the D.I., softly. 'I'd like to be free from a little of this pain.'

That does it. Let's say I've been out-voted. I slip the thong of the blackjack over my wrist, and hold it ready for quick action, then unlock the cuff from the ironwork of the bed, hand the morphine tube to Charlie and tense myself for action, supposing this is some involved try-on.

It isn't.

Back to the circus. Back to the flyers. If Charlie hasn't been beating his gums—if he really *did* fling himself around under the canopy of a big top—common mallum suggests that he's seen accidents. Maybe even been at the receiving end of accidents. Which, in turn, means he knows a little more about dealing with agony than the average citizen. Could be—could *well* be—he's either used these morphine tubes, or seen them used.

Whatever ... he knows the knack.

A tiny squirt, to clear the needle of air. An easing of the arm, until it's in a bent position; until the veins can be the more easily located. A probing with the fingers. A slight pinching, to get the chosen vein a little nearer to the skin surface. Then, concentration ... the whole world, pin-pointed upon that one spot where the needle has to go in. Then the jab—not a slow pushing, like an amateur might do things—but a quick, painless stab which goes just so deep, but no deeper. Then the slow, steady squeeze of the tube, until all the goodnight lotion has been transferred into the blood stream. And, finally, the quick jerk free, leaving a tiny pearl of crimson at the point where the needle went in.

Charlie tosses the empty morphine tube into the fire.

With some reluctance, I say, 'You're good for something, Charlie.'

The D.I. murmurs, 'Thanks, Goodwin,' and, already, I think I notice a drowsiness in his speech.

Charlie holds his hands by his side, and stares at the window. At the weather, beyond the panes.

He says, 'We need a compass.'

I grunt, 'What we don't have, we don't need.'

'In that stuff?'

I pick the kid's mohair coat, from the flagstones, in front of the fire. I toss it towards Charlie, and say, 'You'll need this.'

He says, 'We'll need more than expensive clothes.'

'A little luck, that's all.'

'And, if I refuse?'

'If?' I lift a warning eyebrow.

'I could. I'd be a damn fool, if I didn't.'

'Charlie,' I explain, 'we go together. Don't get any palsy-walsy notions. What I think about you, still goes. We go outside, together. Outside ... if no farther. Any hanky-panky business, and I link you up to something, outside. And you stay there, till I get back ... *if* I get back. By the time I get back—or by the time somebody else reaches you—you'll need a new set of balls. But—if that's what you want ... be my guest, Charlie. You walk, or you freeze ... or, hopefully, starve to death.'

He threads his arms into the mohair coat.

What the hell choice has he?

CHAPTER SEVEN

Some people figure they know what mist is. People who have never been caught on the Tops. They figure mist is something nature cooked up to make them drive a little more slowly; to make them feel a little less comfortable and a little less sure of themselves. It has to do with temperature and water droplets ... that's how the explanation goes. It happens on motorways, and is the cause of multi-car shunt-ups, where radiators kiss bumper bars, and everybody gets a little hot around the collar and slings the blame at every other driver but himself. Its end-product is spoiled dinners, missed appointments and bad tempers ... and, sometimes, smashed bones, broken skulls and morgue slabs.

I tell you ...

Mist, upon these Tops, is a damn sight more than that. It is a cold and clammy killer; a silent, creeping killer which screws certainty to hell, and beyond.

It is a living thing. An all-enveloping ghost, which is never still. It whirls and eddies, it rises and falls, it makes whirlpools in front of your eyes, whirlpools at your feet and other whirlpools above your head. It knocks all sense of balance to blazes; stand perfectly still on what you *know* is flat ground, and you still have to make the effort not to keel over ... because, thanks to this very special mist, either you, or the world, is slipping sideways. An optical illusion? Of course ... but on such a grand scale that it *has* to be believed.

It takes all the will-power in the world to tell this mist that *you* are right, and *it* is wrong.

A lot of people have come to grief in this mist.

The amazing thing is that a lot of people *haven't*!

Add to the mist, the snow. It is never less than calf-deep and, where it has drifted, it comes above the knees. It is not yet frozen, or hard-packed, and the soft, floury wetness puts you off Christmas cards for the rest of your life.

Ten steps, and the farmhouse could be on the far side of the moon, for all we know. Our immediate world is one of a silent, shifting maelstrom of eternal greyness.

'Where, now?' asks Charlie.

His rusty voice sounds different. It is as if he is talking through a pad of cotton waste. Clear enough, but muffled; deadened by the weight of the mist and the cushioning effect of the snow.

The cuffs link his right wrist to my left and, in my right gloved fist, I swing the blackjack.

'The wall,' I say. 'The dry-stone wall. It's to the right. Then the tractor shed ... to get our bearings.'

'Straight ahead,' grunted Charlie.

'Eh?'

'The wall. It's straight ahead. We veered right, when we came out of the door.'

'Oh, for Christ's sake.'

I turn to face him ... which, when you don't know North from Easter Tuesday, is a damn fool thing to do!

We waste time indulging in mild argument. Right, or straight ahead? One of us has to be right, one of us has to be wrong. Nor is it an academic argument. This much, I grant Charlie ... that to point our noses in the wrong direction is something he, too, doesn't favour. And that damn wall will be under snow, by this time. We'll know it's there, when we feel it with our feet ... and not before.

Arguing, at a time like this. At a place like this. In these surroundings. We're both certifiable ... it's like arguing in Hampton Court Maze.

By the time I've threatened to smack him with the black-jack if he disagrees with my sense of direction, it is too late. Hell only knows which way we're now facing.

We turn right—our 'now' right—and lift one leg, then the other, clear of the snow and move forward.

Ten minutes later, Charlie growls, 'Satisfied now, Cameron?'

'We'll hit it at an angle. That's all.'

'You always were a pillock,' he says, with feeling.

'And you should know,' I come back, with equal feeling.

We move forward. Sluggishly, and with snow-heavy shoes and soaked trousers; with the mist clinging web-like to our clothes and eyelashes.

After fifteen minutes, or so, Charlie stops.

'Keep moving,' I mutter.

'Where's the wall, Cameron?' he asks.

'All right. We've missed it. By my reckoning, we're walking parallel with it. We'll still hit the road.'

'And then?'

'We dig the car out. By hand, if necessary. Then, we drive it back to civilisation.'

'You're out of your mind.'

'We drive it,' I snarl. 'If we've to clear a way, on our hands and knees. It's downhill ... and, with luck, the snow-plough might have already cleared a path.'

'You're kidding yourself, Cameron.'

'Shift yourself, Charlie.' I bring the blackjack into view,

threateningly. 'Downhill—that's good enough ... we'll hit the road.'

'We aren't walking downhill,' he says, flatly.

'Don't be such a bloody fool. Of course we're...'

'We're rising. All the time.'

'Don't talk like a...'

'We haven't hit a wall. *Any* sort of a wall.'

He's right. Damn him to hell, he's right! We should have reached one of the dry-stone walls whi_h criss-cross the tops, slightly lower than the farmhouse. They're there. Without real pattern—without real reaso_ ... but *there*. And, by this time, we should have hacked our shins against one of them.

Above the farmhouse ... nothing. No stone walls. Nothing!

Except.

Charlie puts it into words.

He says, 'Laybourne's Leap. If we keep climbing *that's* what we'll hit.'

'We aren't climbing,' I insist ... but I don't sound too sure, because I'm *not* too sure.

Left, right—up, down—north, south, east or west ... who the hell knows? This stuff—this continually moving mist—makes a final mockery of direction. The mist, and the snow. The slope—if there *is* a slope—is a gentle slope, and the sheer graft of humping a way through this thickness of snow makes it as hard to walk downhill as it is to walk up. The infinitesimal pull of gravity is cancelled out.

The truth is, I don't *know*.

The truth is, that Charlie could be so right ... we could be edging our way towards Laybourne's Leap.

Let me tell you about Laybourne's Leap.

It's known in these parts ... but not much farther afield. It's way, and gone to hell, in a rarely visited wilderness. Not as well known as The Strid, near Bolton Abbey. But very much like The Strid.

You know The Strid?

If not, let me tell you.

The River Wharfe. One of the main rivers of Yorkshire. A big river and, for much of its length, a broad river. Except at The Strid.

At The Strid, nature turns very nasty. It squeezes the Wharfe through rocks, which form a broken abyss less than eight feet across. You can hear the roar of the water, long before you reach the cracked and slippery stones; a roar of anguish and anger which turns the timid away from the edge.

The stones which line the lip are moss-covered and wet with spray from the tumbling race. There are notice boards, warning would-be daredevils not to try it. Not to try the leap.

The distance is nothing. Eight feet is nothing of a jump. But the take-off is slimy, and the landing is slimy ... and nobody has yet made it.

Oh, they've tried. The fools. The show-offs. They've tried ... and they've all died. A handful have come to the surface, down river. The rest? The rocks, under all that depth of water, are as ruthless as a Venus Fly Trap. They grab, and they hold, and the black, crazy water strips flesh from bones, then pulverises bones into dust.

The Strid. It is a terrible place. A terrifying place. And the woods around it seem haunted by the shades of idiots, and suicides, who have launched themselves into that short leap to eternity.

Idiots and suicides ... and those who refused to recognise The Strid as one of nature's perfect killers. The nosey ones. The ones who have stood on the edge, looked down ... then slipped.

I know of no Yorkshireman who does not treat The Strid with the respect it both demands and deserves. The Wharfe is a quiet river, a peaceful river and slow to anger —a Yorkshire river ... but, at The Strid, it suddenly explodes into anger, and its anger is homicidal, with no holds barred.

The Strid.

Laybourne's Leap is on a par with The Strid.

No river, at its base, but jagged, flint-edged rocks like dragon's teeth. A local landmark. A geological joke in bad taste. A knife-cut, across the landscape—again, about eight feet wide—and, in places, almost a hundred feet deep, with these rocks grinning up at you and waiting to break your back and mangle your flesh, if you take one step too many.

Why 'Laybourne's Leap'?

I could counter, by asking why 'The Strid'?

No reason at all, other than that it has to be called *something*.

It's killed its quota of sheep. And men ... and a few women. Ramblers and fell walkers. And rock-climbers, to whom that crack in Mother Earth was a challenge.

Brave men!—we-ell, maybe ... may some of them rest in peace!

But, supposing we *are* climbing, it's up there, some-where.

One more damn thing to worry about.

Within the next twenty minutes, the worry gathers

momentum until it becomes something not too far removed from panic. I find I am breathing a little heavier—sweating a little more ... and it is not all from pushing a path through the snow.

We try to keep in step.

How the hell can any two men keep in step, in this stuff, especially when they're linked together by handcuffs? It is like an egg-and-spoon-cum-sack-race, along a course of knee-deep mud.

Like the flicker of gunfire, beyond a distant horizon, the first thoughts of hopelessness dance around at the back of my mind. We have, perhaps, done a crazy thing; we have challenged nature—the savage nature of the Tops—and we are staggering, blindly, towards the only possible end.

And, at lucid moments of objective thought, I come to a bitter conclusion. That this is as it should be. That this is what we both deserve. That the hatred, and the rottenness, and the loathing are all now catching up on us—both of us—and that, very rapidly, the scales of natural justice are levelling themselves out into a perfect balance.

But, most of the time, I am angry.

Anger ...

Could be I left the womb a creature of perpetual anger. Could be anger flows through my body with the blood itself. Could be. This I know, that anger is an emotion which I am rarely without. It is part of me; this bitter, black anger, which for much of the time is directed at the world in general but which can, and so very easily, be concentrated upon a single person, or a single circumstance. Throughout most of my waking hours, I seethe, I rage, I boil with an inner fury. I despise men undeserving of my derision. Shamelessly, and without quali-

fication. That they live is reason enough for my contempt
... and the contempt is the compost heap from which
flowers my never-ending anger.

There are, I suppose, other people like myself in this
world. Men (probably even women) who burn with this
disdain for the rest of mankind. To whom the human
race is little more than a herd of animals of a lower order
than themselves. Who gorge themselves upon their inner
anger, and count pity and compassion wasted emotions.

Why the hell should we pity? Anything, or anybody?

This is a rat-race, friend, and those with the begging
bowls know it. They whimper and whine, and those who
fill their bowls are the fools. But the angry ones ignore
the bowls and, instead, boot the beggars up the arse in
an attempt to jerk some semblance of life into their miserable bodies.

I tell you ... the angry inherit the earth.

The meek only inherit the leftovers.

So, why the hell should we pity?

Why the hell should we even *believe*?

Charlie found Laybourne's Leap.

Which is why I am now spreadeagled in the snow, damn
near smothered in the stuff, and kicking and scratching
with my toes and with my free hand in some sort of an
attempt to find something—anything!—capable of holding
me from following him over the edge.

My left hand feels as if it's being ripped off, at the wrist.
The steel of the handcuff rubs and chafes the skin, as he
pendulums above the jag-toothed rocks which are waiting
to break his back. And—damn him to hell—I'm going
with him ... slowly, I'm being dragged along on my belly,
towards the brink.

How did it happen?

How *do* these things happen?

The mist is mainly to blame. The mist and the snow. Neither of us could see far enough ahead, and the snow had built itself into an overhanging lip, and Charlie stepped onto the edge of the lip.

And that could have been the end of Charlie.

That *would* have been the end of Charlie ... except for the handcuffs.

Now, it could well be the end of us both.

I find the thought slightly amusing. Charlie Goodwin and Ray Cameron, smashed to hell on broken rocks; the double-act to the bitter end; the duo who specialise in ballsing everything to buggery ... and this is the biggest balls-up of all.

Were I not busy trying to stop the gentle slide forward, I might take time off for a quick belly-laugh.

The toe of my right shoe catches on something. Some small irregularity in the rock, under the snow. Some tiny indentation, eaten into the surface by a few thousand years of weather. Not enough to be called a crack, or a groove, or even a miniature cavity. Nothing—but enough ... just.

I jerk every muscle in my right foot and leg, ram the toe of the shoe home and stop sliding. I plaster myself hard into the snow, claw with the fingers of my right hand and kick some sort of leverage into being with my left foot.

Then, I breathe again.

Deep breaths, but gentle breaths. Breaths which (I hope) will not disturb this ridiculously precarious balancing act.

Charlie has stopped penduluming—which helps a little —and has enough gumption to hang there, motionless.

Maybe he's passed out with fright, but I doubt it. Who knows? Who the hell cares?

When I can talk, I talk. Softly. Gently. As if words, too loudly spoken, might disturb the finely tuned game we are playing with eternity.

I say, 'Okay, mastermind. What now?'

'Thank God for the handcuffs.' His voice is quiet, but unhurried. It has a hidden chuckle lurking beneath its surface.

'Without them, you'd be on your way by this time, Charlie,' I agree.

'Another of your mistakes, Cameron.'

'We all make 'em.'

'Fortunately.'

I say, 'Don't let's prolong the *tête-à-tête*.'

'Why? What's holding us?'

'Hope ... and little else.'

'Gently does it, then.' He pauses, then continues, 'This is my show, Cameron. It has to be. I know the technique.'

'A legacy of the big top?' I sneer, into the snow.

'You'd better hope so.'

'What?' I ask.

'A slow chin-up. Smooth. Nothing jerky. Get this, Cameron—get it straight—if it's as fine as you say it is, we can't afford an ounce of extra weight. No sudden drag. Smooth as silk, and we might make it.'

'So bloody easy.'

'*Not* easy. But, just possible ... as long as *you* don't get any brainwaves.'

'Such as?'

'That you can help. That you can do any damn thing at all, except stay perfectly still ... and pray like the clappers.'

'You won't make it, Charlie,' I say, flatly. And, to be honest, I couldn't care less whether, or not, he does.

'Five gets you ten.'

I smile into the snow, and murmur, 'Goodbye Charlie. It's not been too nice knowing you ... but, goodbye.'

And then, he starts the trick.

Honesty demands that I admit my reluctant admiration. It is a magnificent trick, and that his life depends upon it makes it no less magnificent. It is a trick performed in private—in the silence of mist and the solitude of snow —but its performance merits an audience of thousands ... and thunderous applause for its very attempt.

I can't see him, but I know. Every slow-motion movement is transmitted, through the metal of the handcuffs, up my arm and into the imagination of my brain.

He raises his left arm. Slowly. So slowly that not a single flake of snow is disturbed. He raises it in such a manner that, although the weight on my own left wrist shifts, ever so slightly, it doesn't increase by so much as a gramme. The left hand eases up the cuff of my overcoat and jacket, and the fingers close around my right arm. About three inches above the wrist—about three inches above the steel circle of the cuff—and the grip is as firm, and as immovable, as the clamp of a chain-wrench.

There is an exchange; muttered words from behind clenched teeth.

He says, 'Ready? Don't move.'

'Why not?'

'Eh?'

'A quick constitutional ... to work up an appetite.'

'D'you *want* to break your stupid neck, Cameron?'

'Charlie—if I was sure it would break *yours*—cheap at the price.'

'Die, if you must, Cameron,' he snarls, softly. 'Just stay still ... that's all.'

A muttered exchange, which says so little, but means so much. He wants to live. I don't blame him ... who doesn't? But he isn't scared; there isn't one grain of fear in his tone. Plenty of hatred, plenty of disgust and not a little contempt ... but no fear. He's still Charlie Goodwin, the bastard who thinks he can do *anything*. And maybe he's right. Maybe he *can*.

I mutter, 'Get on with it, Charlie. You'll break, before I do.'

He moves his right hand. Gradually. Slow-paced. And the agony of the cuff, biting into my wrist, eases for a moment. Then the fingers grip, beneath the fingers of his left hand, and the bracelet of steel becomes the fulcrum from which he will attempt the dicey part of his crawl from beyond the brink. A fulcrum ... as agonising as a mediaeval torture instrument. A circle of white-hot steel which threatens to burn the end of my arm into a handless stump.

I let loose a quick hiss of pain, then push my teeth together and defy him to get even so much as a grunt out of me.

Charlie Goodwin must never again feed me pain ... must never again *know* that he is feeding me pain. The pain-goblet is filled. One drop more, and it will overflow. It will spill, and then ...

The Coroner clears his throat and, with some embarrassment, says, 'This must be very painful for you, Mr. Cameron. Very distressing.'

I say, 'Yes, sir,' because, in these sort of circumstances, that makes some form of sense; it means damn-all ...

but that, of itself, makes it at least non-controversial.

The Coroner puts on his look of sympathy. His assistant, the jurors, the witnesses. the press-hounds and the coppers follow suit. This is a Coroner's Court, for Christ's sake. Therefore, when H.M.C. looks angry, everybody *looks angry—when he looks outraged,* everybody *looks outraged ... when he looks sympathetic,* everbody *looks sympathetic. He is a puppet-master and, like most Coroners, puffed out with self-importance; the court is his own, personal stage and, when he pulls the strings, all the little people present perform whatever trick he decrees.*

They all assume an air of sad sympathy ... the hypocritical bastards!

The Coroner drones, 'I have your statement here, Mr. Cameron. I'll go through it, with you—summarise it, for the benefit of the jury—and we'll make the deposition as short as possible.'

'Thank you, sir.'

And now, I'm the hypocrite. What the hell am I thanking him for?

He adjusts his spectacles and, with a ballpoint pen, scans the lines of the typewritten quarto. His assistant straightens the deposition form in her typewriter and waits, fingers poised above the keys.

He says, 'You were—er—going on duty. Leaving your house, for the police station. The last time you saw the deceased—your child—Charles Cameron, he was in the house. In the living room. Playing with a toy ... a teddy bear.'

The fingers fly over the keys, and the letter-bars flick up, and back, as the story patters and clacks its way onto the deposition form.

'You went to the garage. Reversed your motor car out

of the garage, and into the drive. Your usual practice. A thing you do almost every day. Your intention was to reverse the car onto the road, park it by the kerb, prior to returning to the house, to say goodbye to your wife and child.'

He pauses, long enough for the assistant to record the words on the deposition; not the exact words he speaks, but the story, told by him, changed as if told by me. Coroners are allowed to play such subtle ploys with the game of truth.

He says, 'The last time you saw your child—saw him alive, that is—he was in the living room, playing with his teddy bear. You didn't see him leave the house. You didn't see him run into the drive, into the path of your reversing motor car. The next thing you knew, you'd struck your child with the rear of the car. Knocked him to the ground. And one of the wheels—the rear, offside wheel—ran over his chest. Death was instantaneous.'

The assistant clicks away, to keep the typewriting in line, as I say, 'I—I didn't know that. I didn't realise he was dead.'

'No. Of course not.' The Coroner smiles official under-standing. 'You did what you could. All any father could have done. You telephoned for an ambulance, but your son was pronounced dead, upon his arrival at the hospital. You've heard the evidence of the pathologist. Death was instantaneous ... your son didn't suffer. Nevertheless, you have the full, and unqualified, sympathy of this court. Now—if you'll step forward, please ... read the deposition, then sign it, if it contains all you wish it to contain.'

I say, 'Thank you, sir,' and step down from the box.

And, at the same time, I try to figure out exactly who

it is who's dead. Just the kid? Or the two of us? Or, maybe, all three of us?

Okay ... one of us is going to go through the curtains of that crematorium. But (the way I see things) we're all three dead, and one of us is already buried.

I, too, am dead ... I'm just not yet ready to have dirt thrown in my face.

Charlie unfolds the fingers of his left hand. He does a slow arm-bend with his right arm; a feat of sheer, controlled muscle-work the like of which I have never before witnessed. It edges his whole body up, above the lip of the brink and, at the same time, gouges the steel of the cuff into my wrist and the upper part of my hand. Could be bones are being broken. Broken slowly, and broken very painfully. I wouldn't know ... and like hell I'm going to tell him.

For the first time, some of the snow shifts. A bite— enough to fill a dinner plate—falls away as his chest brushes the miniature overhang and, for a split second I figure it's all been a wasted effort.

My heart skips a couple of beats, and I hardly dare breathe.

For the first time since he slipped over the edge I see part of his face. It rises, slowly, into my field of vision. The top half of a battered face; bruised and with one eye closed; swollen and soaked with sweat and melted snow. One hell of a face. A face I have cause to hate—a face I undoubtedly *do* hate ... but, at the same time, the face of a man who, during the last few minutes, has driven reluctant admiration deep into that hatred.

Hatred, spiced with admiration ... the craziest brew of all.

I feel the tremor—the ever so slight tremble—of his right arm as the muscles grow weary of the near-impossible pull, followed by the equally near-impossible hold.

Like a languidly moving snake, his left arm moves up and over the brink. It catches the snow, and a second dollop dislodges itself from the overhang and drops into the chasm. The arm continues to move up. It touches my right shoulder, and the fingers crawl across my shoulder-blades, then fasten themselves onto the material of my overcoat at my left armpit.

And now, his whole face is in view and there is a definite shake on his right arm.

'When I say,' he gasps. 'Bend your left arm ... slowly. Don't pull. Don't try to help. Let me do the work. Just don't hinder. Then, when I say—not before, but when I say "Now"—roll away from the edge ... fast. Understand?'

'I'm not dumb,' I grind, from behind clenched teeth.

'That's only an opinion.'

'Maybe ... but *I* didn't fall down the bloody hole.'

The grin is a grimace, as he croaks, 'Right. Start bending your arm.'

I bend it and, as I bend it, he straightens his own right arm; pushing himself higher from the fulcrum of the cuff around my left wrist and hand until, gradually, his centre of gravity shifts. The grip of his left hand tightens at my armpit and, suddenly—almost unexpectedly—he is there ... like a see-saw, and able to topple forward, with the pull of his left hand.

He yells, *'Now!'* and, as I roll, he rolls with me. Awkwardly. Slithering, rolling and flailing at the snow until we both sprawl, utterly exhausted, in the cold, wet, beautiful eiderdown of whiteness.

Gradually—like liquid working its way through litmus paper—the truth drips through. We've made it. We actually *have* knitted fog. We actually *have* built ourselves a seaworthy, barbed-wire canoe. We actually *have* pole-vaulted the moon.

Christ!

As of this moment, nothing—but *nothing*—is imposs-ible.

I turn my head, and glance at Charlie.

Sweet Jesus, he looks like something a pack of hounds have fought over. He looks ugly; he never looked hand-some, but now he looks positively horrific. That mangled face, with its gaping mouth gulping in air. The mohair overcoat; soaked and soiled, and shredded down one sleeve —and much of the soiling is blood ... my blood.

I shift my eyes and, for the first time, look at my left wrist.

Hell's bells ... I want to puke

Like a glove which is about to be peeled from the hand, the skin and the top flesh have been parted from the upper wrist to the root of the thumb. Rolled down—almost neatly—until there is a thick band of meat and skin, which forms a bracelet and, into this bracelet, the steel of the handcuff is still embedded. Here, and there, the white of bone peeps through the crimson. Skinned alive— the thought quick-silvers through my mind ... one of those silly snippets of half-learned history. The old-time torture chamber; the iron maiden, the thumbscrew, the branding irons ... and the business of being skinned alive. This must be a small taste of it. A quick lick of the lollipop ... and it is not a very nice lollipop.

There is much blood ... but, for the moment, the pain is gone. Only numbness remains. Numbness, and the sight of it, and the sight of it makes me want to puke.

I don't puke. Instead, I start laughing. Not honest laughter; not the laughter created by good comedians; not the laughter which bubbles up as a result of humorous writing. False laughter. Laughter from hell itself. Hysterical laughter, which one part of my mind loathes, but which is beyond my control.

Charlie, too, laughs.

We sprawl. We throw our arms as wide as the cuffs will allow. We open our mouths, and we howl into the swirling mist.

Between us, we've taken on Old Nick. We've twisted his tail, de-horned him and taken his trident and rammed it up his arse. That's what we've done ... and that's why we laugh.

That's the sort of laughter it is; the laughter of temporary madness.

Then, like the drop of a guillotine, the laughter stops. We're back to Square One ... and, once more, we detest each other.

'Downhill,' croaks Charlie, sneeringly.

'Forget it.'

'We were going to reach the car ... remember?'

'Forget it,' I repeat.

'All we had to do was keep the wall on our right.'

'Anybody could have ...'

'Which bloody wall?'

'We're alive,' I growl. 'Be grateful for small mercies.'

'We're alive,' he echoes, contemptuously.

'That's what I said.'

'But, no thanks to *you*, Cameron.'

'You're the one who fell down the bloody Leap.'

'You're the stupid sod who led us to it.'

'Not deliberately, for Christ's sake. I didn't...'

'You're never wrong, Cameron. You never *were* wrong.'

'All right. I made a mistake.'

'One hell of a mistake.'

'Anybody could have...'

'No!' he snarls.

'You're infallible. Is that it?'

'I know these Tops.'

'Oh, my God, yes. After all these years, you...'

'I know where Laybourne's Leap is.'

'You do *now*,' I sneer.

'Watch it, Cameron,' he warns. 'I've had as much of you as I'm going to stand.'

'Charlie,' I say, flatly. 'You're going to have as much of me as I can give you. As much as I feel like giving you ... which is a lot. I've a whale of lost time to make up for, Charlie, old-pal-old-pal. I've a lot of bile to work out of my system. And you're going to get it. Every ounce of it ... with interest. So-o, don't tell *me* what you're going to take. You're going to take the lot!'

'Assuming you're big enough.'

'For ten bastards like you,' I snarl.

And then, we fight.

Fight! Judas Christ, was there ever such a mockery of a set-to? Kneeling, facing each other—neither of us has the strength to stand upright—and hampered by the handcuffs. Up to the chest in snow, and rasping for breath we haven't yet regained. We swing at each other and, nine times out of every ten, we miss. And when we connect—I swear!—we haven't the strength to knock a sparrow from its perch.

The hatred is there. We'd each kill the other, had we the strength. But the flesh isn't just weak ... it's damn near non-existent. There isn't a school-ma'am who, at this moment, couldn't pan us both before dumping us in a corner, like naughty boys.

It lasts maybe five minutes ... maybe less.

Charlie drops his arms. No—I'm doing him an injustice ... he tries to raise them, but can't. He just lets them hang, with the hands on the surface of the snow.

Me? I haven't the muscle power left to lift the hand which is linked to his right wrist. I try one last right swing, but the arm flops, before the fist is within twelve inches of Charlie's face.

'Later,' I whisper, between gasps.

'Yeah.' He manages a weak nod, as he chokes for air.

'I'll rip blue shit out of you, Charlie.'

'Yeah ... if *I* stand still, and let you.'

'You never could...'

'I can *now*, Cameron.'

'You think,' I pant.

But I know what he means. Deep down, and despite the exhaustion, I know that on level terms he can now take me apart. Time was, he couldn't. Time was when I had the slight edge ... maybe. But not now. Maybe all the circus crap *wasn't* crap, after all. It follows. That trick of hauling himself out of the Leap wasn't some extempore show-off. It needed skill. It needed real muscle and, moreover, very controlled muscle. The sort of muscle flyers *might* need.

And another thing ...

He has taken some pan-handling, since yesterday morning. He has taken some thump, and absorbed some punishment. Okay—his face shows it ... but, inside, he isn't licked. Inside, he hasn't yet been touched.

Over the years—and for whatever reason—Charlie Goodwin has grown very tough. Not 'tearaway' tough. Not 'roustabout' tough. *Tough!* ... the real thing. Like teak. Like perfectly tempered steel.

I ponder the problem as we both work to get our lungs functioning, again.

I come to a conclusion, and the conclusion (in military lingo) is that, until now, I have underestimated the enemy.

We haul ourselves to our feet and, without another word, start the stagger back to the farmhouse.

CHAPTER EIGHT

It isn't difficult ... finding the farmhouse, I mean.

The mist is still around, and as thick as ever; the Empire State Building could be twenty yards away, but we wouldn't see it, in this stuff. But, thick as the mist is, we can always see one stride ahead of us, and one stride ahead of us there is always a couple of holes in the snow, with a concave trudge-mark leading us to each hole, supposing we have any doubts. Footprints. The way we came ... whichever way *that* was.

We go back the same way. Could be we stumble triple the distance needed ... I wouldn't argue. I just don't know. Neither of us know. But, if it's *thirty* times the distance needed, who cares? At the end—when we reach the end—there is shelter, there is rest, there is food and there is warmth.

Basics. That's all we're reaching for. Basics ... which, at this moment, are luxuries.

The gore still pours from my wrist, runs down my fingers and makes pretty patterns on the surface of the snow, as we move forward. Irregularly spaced crimson beads, of differing sizes, linked by a scarlet thread. A red necklace, which disappears into the mist, behind us.

I ease the metal clear of the flesh—twist it, as gently as I can, and pull, like a butcher pulling a skewer from raw meat—and it hurts ... it hurts like hell. I think I never knew what physical pain really was until this moment.

Until I pull the steel of the bracelet from its enveloping flesh.

I should, I suppose, throw up. At the pain, and at the sight ... I could, I suppose, be excused were I to bring up my guts.

I don't.

Charlie is here ... and something tells me that, in similar circumstances, Charlie would have plucked the metal from the bleeding meat, stonefaced and without a murmur. Could be I'm wrong—could be that, mentally, I'm beginning to build this bastard up into something of a superman ... but I think not. Nineteen years in this job, and 'supermen' have long been given the bum's rush to the bottom of the garden, with all the other fairy-folk.

Nevertheless—and because Charlie is here, alongside me—I swallow agony, like it is good Scotch whisky, and put a concrete plug on my stomach contents.

The cuff comes clear, and what is left doesn't look too nice. My wrist looks as if it is wearing a broad charm-band of fresh pig's offal.

A thought lodges itself in my mind.

'How come?' I ask.

'What?' He asks the counter-question, without looking at me. Without pausing in his bent-kneed push forward from one footprint to the next.

I say, 'My wrist is chewed to hell. Yours isn't even marked.'

'The links,' he grunts.

'Eh?'

'I grabbed the links ... that's all. One of us had to do the work. One of us had to carry the aggro. I chose the work.'

It answers the question. Standard handcuffs ... British

style. The two bracelets are joined by a three-link chain; two normal, steel links and a centre swivel-link. There is space—*just* enough space—to twist the wrist and grip the triple-link which joins the twin circles of steel.

'Nice going,' I sneer. 'You still know the easy way.'

'I chose the work,' he repeats. 'You couldn't have *done* the work. We'd have hung there till the crows had breakfast from our eyeballs.'

'Charlie, whatever *you* can do, I can...'

'Stop kidding yourself, Cameron.'

'You think?'

'I *know*.'

'Tell the judge, Charlie. He'll enjoy the laugh.'

'I'll do that. If we ever reach the judge.'

I don't argue. It is standard tough talk, learned and delivered by every street-corner muscle-boy. Like whistling in a haunted house. Like saying 'I'm going to live another hundred years', when they're screwing the lid into position.

It means nothing. Every cop hears it, a dozen times a week ... and it *always* means nothing.

I fiddle around, until I locate a moderately clean handkerchief from my pocket, then, without pausing in the stumble of our forward push through the snow, I cover the blood-dripping muck which circles my left wrist. The handkerchief keeps the steel clear of the flesh, and not for all the pain in the world—not for all the pearls in the Japanese Ocean—am I going to unlock the handcuffs.

It takes us maybe a million years to reach the farm.

More than once—maybe a score of times—I've been half-convinced (and a little *more* than half-convinced) that we have, once more, screwed things up. The walking-

round-in-circles gag is no gag ... not up here. It happens.
It happens in broad daylight, in high summer. Idiots who
challenge these Tops, without the basic safety of a compass, have walked themselves to death, before today. Come
winter—come the snow, come the mist—and it is almost
a monthly break in the monotony ... some lunatic has
to be found (dead, or alive) and the rescue crowd clicks
into action, and waits around until the weather gives them
an even break.

We have had one tiny piece of luck on our side. The
snow has held off.

Had the snow come—had the foot-holes been filled in
with a fresh fall—somebody, somewhere, would already
be busy tuning up a couple of new harps ... or, maybe,
testing a couple of shovels for balance.

But the snow has held off, and we've made it. The
farmhouse comes up at us, out of the moving mist. It is
an optical illusion, of course, but the impression is there;
that the grey-stone surface of the farmhouse is actually
coming forward, to meet us, out of this ever-shifting mist.

And (I tell you, friend) at this particular moment, the
London Hilton comes a very ropey second to this cen-
turies-old, broken-down hunk of isolated, non-mod-con
architecture.

As I reach for the door, I gasp, 'We made it, Charlie.'

'*We* made it?'

'Don't give yourself bloody airs, boy. You're not im-
mortal.'

He grins a one-eyed, lop-sided sneer, and says, 'I'm a
survivor, Cameron. I *always* make it.'

CHAPTER NINE

Lots of things, I don't know. Lots of answers, I can't give. But one thing for sure, I can recognise Old Man Death when he gets to within touching distance.

I've seen too many stiffs, and too many soon-to-be-stiffs. Something goes, and what was once there is replaced by something else. Don't ask me to be more specific ... just *something*.

It pinches the nostrils. It does a conjuring trick upon the complexion; as if the process of dying starts with the skin, then gradually works inwards, until the job's complete. It affects the eyes, and the lips; as if they, too, feel the first gentle touch of the scythe. The eyes aren't frightened—they aren't resigned—they aren't sad—they aren't tranquil ... they aren't *anything*. They're just eyes. Maybe they can still see. Maybe they are fogging over a little. Maybe they are already blind or, if not blind, beyond registering a non-cockeyed version of what they see to the brain. Maybe anything—but, whatever, they're just eyes ... not yet dead, but fast dying. The lips aren't there any more. Not as lips. They have the colour of the rest of the face ... which is the colour of decaying plaster, tinged with pastel blues and washed out greens. There are no lips. There is merely a slit in the face, which is a mouth.

There is also (and very often) a blessing.

There is no pain. It is as if the frame of a dying man

has used up all the pain it was born with. As if pain is a quantitative thing; as if we all have a measured amount of suffering to live through and, at the end, all that suffering has been expended ... and we can die empty of all agony.

All this ... but, also, more.

Animals know, by instinct, when they're dying, and man is one more animal—no different and, in the final analysis, no less instinctive than his fellow-animals—and he, too, knows.

The D.I. knows.

He watches the door, as we enter. He tries to hoist himself into a more upright position, on the bed ... fails, and falls back with a sad smile of apology touching his mouth corners.

His eager expression asks a question, and I answer it, without demanding what energy he'd need to voice it.

I say, 'No go, sonny. We took a few wrong turnings. We'll try again, when the mist clears.'

What else? What the hell *else* can I say to a dying man? What further comfort can I give ... without making myself a liar.

I steer Charlie into the scullery and, for the first time, notice the stench. It is bog-smell, and it comes from the scullery and, when we get there, we both know why.

Charlie breathes, 'Holy cow!'

I know exactly what he means ... and he is not remarking upon the pong. He is eyeing the excrement, and the torn pieces of paper, alongside the rear door; he is voicing his wonderment at the sheer guts of a man who, rather than empty his bowels onto a bed, will drag mangled legs across two rooms in a suicidal attempt to prove that he is fully house-trained.

The D.I. is dying, and this is *why* he is dying. Because he wanted a shit, and because I wasn't around to carry him outside.

I unlock the cuff from my own injured wrist, link Charlie to his pet water-pipe, then go back to the main room ... and go a little mad.

'What the hell!' I bawl. 'Is this the sort of crap they feed you at New Scotland Yard? That clean bedclothes are a damn sight more important than human life? Your life, sonny. *Your* miserable little life ... something I've gutted myself for, ever since we reached these Tops. Those flaming legs of yours ... whose fault are they? Who was the brainless bastard who stood there, and waited for Goodwin to shoot 'em from under you? *Who?* You have been a pain in the arse, Mr. Detective Inspector. Get that straight. You've been a pain in the arse, from the moment you arrived. From the moment you stepped off the train. I've wet-nursed you, every inch of the bloody way. *Me!* Detective Constable Cameron ... and you a blasted D.I. from the gold-plated mob itself.

'You're an idiot, sonny. D'you know that? A bloody *idiot*. That animal in there—that cannibal, who tried to shoot your legs off—damn and blast it, you're on *his* side. You're helping *him*. Arsing and farting around—doing everything by the book—so bloody sure that because he didn't spill blood on the bank raid he's some sort of bloody boy scout ... *you've helped him*! He is a bastard. A germ. A shithouse of the first order ... but you wouldn't be told.

'And now *this*. Not wanting to soil your flaming nappies. What the stinking, rotten, stupid, gob-sucking play was *that*? What the...'

I close my mouth, and close my eyes.

I clench my fists against my upper thighs, and don't

even feel the pain from my right wrist.

And why?

Because who the hell am *I* to deny this young kid his puny dignity? Who the hell am *I* to bawl him out, in bargee language, when all he wanted was to be civilised? Who the hell am *I* to pass judgement?

Who the hell am I?

I open my eyes and, for the first time for years, I feel true shame.

The kid is looking up at me. He is on his way out of this world—that fact is so obvious, it hardly needs saying —and he is weeping silently. Not from pain. Not from fear. But, like the kid he is, because he has been given an undeserved tongue-lashing by an older man ... by a man almost old enough to be his father.

I lower myself to my knees, alongside the bed; the stones are hard, but my legs are numb from the cold of the last few hours and, for all I know, I could be kneeling on swansdown. I ease him up from the pillow. Gently; as gently as I would my own son. I embrace his shoulders with my arm, and draw him towards my chest. The weeping stops—the tears no longer build up in those expressionless eyes—and he snuggles his greying face into the soaked material of my overcoat.

What matter that my clothes are saturated? What matter that they have the temperature of iced-water? What matter that I pass some of my physical misery onto him?

He is well beyond the point of feeling either pain or pleasure. His only remaining want is for comfort. Comfortable words. The comforting knowledge that he is not alone ... that, at this moment, he has at least one friend, who will stay and not be afraid.

I tighten my arm a little, lower my cheek onto the

top of his bowed head and croon words of near-affection.

I say, 'Hang on, kid. This is one of the rough spots ... that's all. We'll work our way through it, between us. Up there—above the mist—that old sun is on our side. He's working like the clappers. He'll shift this muck. Just give him time. Then it'll be clear, and they'll be out looking for us. Choppers, rescue teams ... the lot. They're down there, somewhere. In the valley. Ready and waiting. They'll come ... they'll come in time. They'll get us out of this place. I swear. So, hang on, kid. I'm around. I'll stay. All you have to do is fight—sweat it out ... make damn sure they aren't going to have a wasted journey.'

That sort of garbage. That sort of crap. That's what I say, and maybe he hears me ... and maybe he even believes me.

I rock him gently, as I talk.

What else?

He's a kid. He's a baby. He's tired, and wants to sleep ... the last sleep of all. He wants it, like everybody wants it, when it arrives. He wants it—but not alone ... and that small favour I'll willingly grant him.

So, what else? ... From a practical point of view, he is already dead.

He is already dead. Having eased him gently, from the front of the rear, offside wheel, I hold him in my arms. But he is already dead. I don't need medical verification. I don't need a death certificate. I don't need a post mortem examination. I know!

The tyre bounced a path across his tiny chest ... and that did it.

He hangs here, cradled in my arms, with his neck loose and his head flopping and, from a corner of his mouth, a trickle of blood is already working a path towards one of his eyes.

He's dead!

And, how the hell am I going to break the news? How the hell am I going to tell her? What sort of lies must I invent?

The detective inspector from New Scotland Yard dies at twenty-three minutes past two o'clock, in the afternoon. At that time, *exactly*.

He takes a deep, deep breath and, as he releases life with a last exhalation, he mutters a woman's name. The name isn't important. It could be the name of his wife. It could be the name of his daughter. It could be the name of his mother. For all I know, it could be the name of a half-forgotten broad who once gave him the screw of a lifetime ... it's been known.

Just a name ... the last word he speaks, before he starts to stiffen.

I check the time. I'm a copper, and I know there'll be an inquest, and an enquiry. Cold-blooded lunatics who have never lived through this sort of situation will ask questions, and demand answers. Nit-picking questions which, to them, will be all-important. They'll demand pin-pointed answers to their nit-picking questions and, if they don't get the answers, they'll raise dust. They'll anchor their fat backsides to comfortable chairs, behind expensive desks, and they'll glare their ridiculous displeasure ... because, when a man died in my arms, I was too busy feeling sad to itemise and tabulate every fiddling little detail of his death.

It won't be enough that, although he died without pain, he died *because* of pain. They'll want the in's and the out's

—the why's and the wherefore's—and they'll want a description, as detailed and as split-second as an outer-space blast-off.

So, that's why—that's why I know the exact time—fourteen-twenty-three hours ... and I'll tell them, and they'll nod their gormless satisfaction, and they might even congratulate me upon my 'powers of observation'.

But the name—the last word he spoke ... that didn't happen. That was very private. Very secret. And, as far as the brass is concerned, he died without saying a thing.

He wasn't talking to them. He wasn't even talking to *me*. It was maybe a 'goodbye' ... but, for all I know, it could, equally easily, have been a 'hello'. Whatever, it was just a word—a name—which isn't for publication. Which isn't for public discussion. It belongs to *him* ... and I'll not rob him of it, for the sake of a stinking enquiry held by plastic-brained lunatics whose feelings begin, and end, with a filled belly.

I ease him back onto the pillow. I straighten his ruffled hair a little and cover his arms, before I smooth out the blanket. With the first and middle fingers of my right hand I ease the lids over his staring eyes. Gently ... as gently as I'd want him to handle mine.

I murmur, 'You made a cock of it, kid, but you've made amends. Not a squawk. Rest easy, kid ... You're a full-sized man.'

CHAPTER TEN

I try to forget the D.I. To sit around and mourn his passing would do no good, therefore I try to forget him. At first, it isn't easy ... but it gets easier as I busy myself with more urgent matters.

I shed my soaking overcoat, and that, itself, is no small problem. The left wrist of mine has reclaimed centre-stage, and working it slowly out of the wet-heavy overcoat sleeve is a little like cutting off my own hand with a blunt knife. It hurts ... and that is the understatement of the century!

Then, I ease my left hand to the inside of my jacket—above the fastened link-button—make-believe my arm is in a sling and work one-handed. I try a trick; a trick I have tried and pulled in the past, when pain has been part of this job of mine. I work to make my mind forget that part of my body which hurts. To forget it—to ignore it—and, if the trick works, the pain, too, is forgotten ... and the pain goes away. It has worked in the past. When, as a result of a rough-house, the villains have bent my ribs or thumped my skull ... in the past, and in such circumstances, the trick has worked.

But not this time.

This time it is a little like trying to ignore a bleeding stump. This time the torment is bigger than the will-power.

So—okay—I work one-handed ... and I hurt.

The place is getting cold. The fire-grate is choked with ash, the flames have died and the solid heart of embers needs air.

I use one of the thinner logs to clear a draught-way through the bars; rattling the dead ash into the steel tray, beneath. Then I open the door, return to the fire, use my hat as a guard against the hot tray, and carry the ash into the outside mist. I throw it onto the snow, and it hisses and steams, and gives off a pungent sulphur-like smell.

Then, back to the fire with the tray—back to the door, to close it against a dank cold which, by this time, has driven its teeth deep into the marrow of my bones ... and, already, I'm realising the until-now unconsciously accepted advantage of being born with two hands. A full compliment of paws saves both time and footwork.

The embers are already looking more healthy. The new supply of oxygen has boosted a dull red into a gently pulsating orange, with that thin, transparent blue aura which preludes real heat.

Still working one-handed, I arrange logs and cobs in a carefully stacked pyramid, around and above the growing glow. I need warmth. I need something to counter the goose-flesh which periodically makes my whole body tremble; something to stop the chatter of my teeth; something to drive out the ice, and bring back the blood-flow.

God only knows what my body temperature is. Thermometers are at a premium up here, in this wild place. But it must be low—dangerously low—and, although much of the drop is due to recent exposure some, at least, is due to shock. The interlude of polemics up at Laybourne's Leap is guaranteed to have some sort of back-lash, and the tearing of the flesh at the wrist can't have helped. That thing on the bed died, not merely from pain—not merely from loss of blood—but also from shock. Shock is a silent killer—I'm no medic, but I know *that* ... and the D.I. isn't going to have a D.C. to accompany him on his journey to the final Interview Room.

Whatever else, I must get warm.

Having fixed the fire, I go into the scullery and clean up the mess near the rear door.

Why?

Not for reasons of hygiene; in this sort of situation, dirt and smell is of very secondary importance. I do it (I suppose) as a final favour to a young detective inspector who choked on the mouthful he'd bitten off. I do it for him. It seems logical ... almost obvious. If the kid was prepared to kill himself in an attempt to reach the outside of that door, the least I can do—the least *anybody* could do—is carry what he wanted to rid himself of those last few feet.

I clean up the mess, and Charlie watches me.

As I move around the scullery, I skirt the walls. I stay beyond Charlie's grab, and Charlie notices it, and smiles, secretly, to himself. Okay—let him smile ... with this one as a pet, who needs an anaconda? Charlie I can deal with, later. For the moment I have more important problems to sort out.

Nevertheless, I worry a little.

I have already decided that the new Charlie is not the Charlie I once knew. He is tougher. Harder. Fitter. In the old days, he was no jelly-baby—he could take 'em, as fast as they were thrown at him—and maybe I could lick him, but maybe I couldn't. In the old days. But, *now*. I have the gut-feeling that the steam is coming back to him a damn sight faster than it is coming back to *me*. His smashed face is growing no less ugly, his closed eye remains closed ... but, unlike me, the shakes haven't touched him. He squats on the stone floor, and mocks me with his good eye. Without saying a word, he warns me ... let me drop my guard the breadth of a single hair, and he'll have me. He'll tear me apart, and scatter me to the winds. And, what's more, he *can*—or thinks he can ... and I have this gut-feeling that maybe he isn't kidding himself.

While I do my housework in the scullery, Charlie worries me a little.

I return to the main room.

The fire is dancing and belching out heat, and the temperature is getting much more comfortable. I ease off for a few minutes; stand with my back to the blaze—feet wide and backside taking the full blast of life-giving warmth—and, very gradually, I begin to feel a little less like a drowned rat.

And now, comes the big moment.

The wrist.

Something has to be done with it. I need that hand, again ... if only to deal the pasteboards when we're killing time, playing pontoon in the small hours, back at the nick. I need that hand and, unless I iron out the irregularities of that flesh—and before much longer—the odds are in favour of me ending up with something not much more useful than a grappling iron.

First, I must remove the jacket.

Easy—'Slip off your jacket, and make yourself comfortable' ... that's what friends always say. But not this time, buster. This time, the removal of that jacket is likely to be something not too far removed from a heart transplant ... and without anaesthetic!

The wrist reminds me of this. It throbs, like a rubber hose caught in a threshing machine.

I get this big idea. To cut the sleeve clear of my hand and arm with my pocket knife. Nothing to it. That way I keep the heavy material of my jacket away from my injured wrist and hand.

Easy ... in a pig's ear!

I unbutton the jacket. In slow-motion time I lower the left arm until it hangs, slack, by my side, and this is my first mistake. The hand—the whole arm—seems to have doubled its weight. The impression is that it has suddenly become filled with liquid metal. Hot metal. And the furnace which is keeping the metal in a liquid condition is right there, at the wrist. I work hard to convince myself that this is imagination run riot, while I fumble the knife from my pocket.

Then comes the contortion bit.

To work the right arm clear of its sleeve—the jacket clear of my shoulders—without allowing the weight to fall down the left sleeve and tear my suffering hand from its moorings.

I figure it might be easier—safer—sat down, so I sit on the edge of the bed. And there, for all of five sweating minutes, I do an escapologist act, with the base of my spine nudging the ribs of a stiffening corpse. I find that my calculations are correct. It is possible to do this thing ... just! It is not easy. Doing a four-minute mile in clogs might have been preferable.

However, it gets done, and now comes the knife-and-teeth act.

Have you ever tried it? On films—on the T.V.—in books —the hero pulls the trick almost off-handedly. He grabs the blade between his teeth, and opens the knife. Fine— if you have teeth like a horse ... but I haven't. I sweat some more, I curse some more but, eventually, I make it

... and only God and all His angels know how I do it without carving myself a spare mouth.

The rest is easy ... like hell it's easy!

This jacket of mine is made of good Harris tweed, and this knife of mine was never meant to cut this class of cloth. To even puncture the material sends oscillations of excruciating pain down my arm to my wrist. To saw a way the whole length of the sleeve would be more than I could ever take. Which leaves the seams. I start at the shoulder and, stitch at a time, part first the outer tweed, then the lining, of the sleeve from the rest of the jacket. Then, still stitch at a time, down the sleeve and down the lining of the sleeve.

It takes almost thirty minutes but, when it's done, I can ease the injured wrist clear of the arm-hole and, although I've ruined a good jacket, I'm content in the knowledge that what I've done couldn't have been done with less agony.

I roll up the sleeve of my shirt, survey the knotted handkerchief around the wrist and hand, and decide upon my next move.

The blood from the wound has congealed. The final act of removing the handkerchief calls for a certain amount of cunning.

Water—that, for sure ... water, with which to liquefy the congealed blood. And warm water—water at normal blood-heat ... that, I decide, is the best way.

I light the primus. One-handed, and with my injured hand still hanging at my side. A tricky operation—but, by this time, I'm fast becoming an expert at dealing with tricky operations ... the measuring of the methylated spirit, the lighting of the spirit with a brand from the now-roaring fire, the positioning of the stove on the flagged floor and, when the moment arrives, the holding of the stove steady with one foot, while I pump up the paraffin pressure with my good hand.

Back to the scullery and, still keeping out of Charlie's reach—still not exchanging a word with him—I take the pan in which, yesterday, I boiled the knife's spike prior to a makeshift operation which was wasted. I position the pan under the snout of the pump and, leaning sideways across the sink, in order to keep clear of the bastard responsible for my pain, I work the pump handle awkwardly, but well enough to fill the pan almost to its brim.

Back in the main room, I stand the pan on the flame of the stove and, using my teeth and uninjured hand, rip the sleeve-lining of my jacket into swabbing pieces.

Understand me. I am no pansy. I am no petunia, ready to wilt and knock off for the season unless I am nursed and molly-coddled into continuing a beautiful existence. I know myself well enough to recognise that I am more animal than aesthetician. I belong to a treeless jungle, whose undergrowth crawls with human snakes; a jungle peopled with more than its fair share of man-eaters; a jungle where the kill-or-be-killed law rules supreme. And, in this jungle, I have earned a reputation. I can dish it out ... but I can also take it. The two go together; glass jaws being something the other animals look for and rejoice in finding.

I call myself a good cop, and I speak no less than the truth. By *my* yardstick, I *am* a good cop. The object of the exercise—the object of *my* exercise—is to hammer 'em stupid. To play them at their own game, and smash the bastards. To tame them ... not train them. To terrorise them, if necessary. To chase them off the streets or. if they won't run, leave them bleeding and defeated, in the nearest gutter.

The Civil Rights crowd object to this brand of law-enforcement.

That's okay by me ... I object to the Civil Rights crowd.

When I stroll a pavement, *I'm* king of that pavement. Me! Not some muscle-heavy yob and his surrounding galaxy of tearaways. I walk in a straight line ... and they either part, or get trampled underfoot.

It's a technique. A very old-fashioned technique. An increasingly unpopular technique, as far as the candy-floss do-gooding outfits are concerned. They (in their infinite unwisdom) would pat the gooney-birds on the head, steer them to the nearest café, feed them coffee and cigarettes and ask them soft-sugar questions; enquire into their *reasons* for committing robbery—for committing rape—for committing murder ... and, from the lying answers received, build a false edifice of excuse.

Which is why I'm still only a detective constable.

The excuses don't interest me. The bastards are guilty and, all the shyster evidence to the contrary, they *stay* guilty until *I* decide they're innocent ... and I never allow myself to change my mind more than once a year!

Tough?

It's a tough world, friend, and mine is a tough profession ... and I pride myself upon being a very tough hombre.

Until this particular moment in time. At this particular moment in time, I would give much to be able to run home to momma. I have been threaded through the meat-grinder ... backwards. I have been boned, chewed up and spat out. I am, in a word, knackered ... and this damn wrist of mine is putting the finishing touch on things, by giving me neon-lit hell.

I sit on the edge of the bed, smoke a cigarette, and take an occasional swig from the whisky bottle.

Maybe I'm feeling a little sorry for myself.

Horse-sense suggests that the water in the pan should reach blood-heat from the top end. That it should be allowed to boil for a few minutes, first, then be allowed to cool ... that way, it might be a little less unclean.

Or, again, maybe I'm finding excuses. Maybe I'm finding reasons for postponing something I'm not looking forward to.

Whatever ... I sit there, watch the surface of the water until it starts to bubble, let it bubble a while, then remove it from the primus.

Ten minutes later—thereabouts—I test the temperature with the little finger of my good hand, and decide the heat is just about right.

I kneel on the floor, with the pan in front of me, and using a torn piece of sleeve-lining, trickle warm water onto the blood-clotted handkerchief around my wrist. I use plenty of water. Water is cheap, and the warmth seems to soothe a little of the pain away. I soak the handkerchief —I soak it well—and that, too, is a mistake.

It is a mistake, because the first job is to untie a knot ... and the knot was tied with all the savagery of the moment of this morning. I should have untied the knot, while the handkerchief was dry. Before I started the soaking process. As it is, it is not easy. The saturated linen seems to have swollen—seems to have tightened—and, eventually, I have to use the spike from the pocket knife to even *start* the knot on its way to being unravelled. I merely repeat myself when I say that the operation increases the agony, but I repeat myself for a good and sufficient reason ... because, with this brand of pain, repetition is not repetition, it is an underlining of the ever-present obvious.

It takes me maybe a quarter of an hour to untie the knot and, by that time, the water has lost most of its heat.

I turn down the flame of the primus, lift the pan once more onto the stove, and continue the soaking process with water which is gradually getting warmer ... and redder.

The handkerchief becomes soggy mush. The steady trickle of water, back into the pan, becomes more scarlet-tinged and slowly—ever so slowly—the material separates itself from the frayed flesh.

I lift the handkerchief clear. Gently. I sling it into the fire, where it first hisses, then blackens, then burns.

Finally, I look at my wrist and hand.

Judas Christ!

I have seen worse messes ... but not often, and not many, and never on my own meat.

A collar of raw flesh and shredded skin has been rolled down, from above the knuckle-bone of the wrist to the root of the thumb and all the way around the hand. A polo-neck of living tissue—*my* living tissue—above which can be seen the sheen of exposed bone, the silver thread of tendons, the ooze of blood and the already gathering pus of suppuration.

Question ... what, in the name of all hell, do you do with chewed-up mash like this?

What I do is very basic, and just about the most heroic thing I've done in my life. I dip the fingers of my good hand into the heating water then—very objectively—pick,

pull, ease and knead the flesh of my wrist into a more-
or-less replacement of where it should be. I start slowly.
I start gingerly. I start with the intention of causing myself
as little extra pain as possible ... but it doesn't work that
way. To touch it—and however lightly—causes screaming
agony, and I suddenly realise that pain is finite. It has
wide limits but, nevertheless, it *does* have limits. The
world may spin a little—turn a little hazy—around the
edges of your vision. A sound like an approaching
express train may build up, between your ears. But the
pain doesn't actually increase. It merely continues along
the same high, nerve-tearing note.

For me, it hit that note at a touch, regardless of how
gossamer light that touch, and it kept that same note ...
regardless of how much I plucked, and picked, and pulled.
No more, and no less. The same note—no louder and no
higher ... just that, in time, it drills tiny holes in your
brain.

Forget the holes, and you end up with a great consola-
tion. You end up with a form of comfort; that all you
must do is retain consciousness, hold down your guts and,
if you can do these two things well enough, you can work
your own flesh back into something like normal shape.

I can do it ... if I can be objective enough. If I can
push back the spinning darkness. If I can clamp my teeth,
until the muscles around my jaws begin to ache with
cramp.

I can do it!

And, brother, I'd *better* damn well do it ... unless I'm
prepared to live out the rest of my life short-handed.

I do it.

I'm sweating like a pig. I'm breathing like I've just won
a fifty mile race. The world has stopped spinning and,

instead, is climbing and swooping, like an old-time, fair-ground shamrock ... but I do it.

I mutter, 'Up you, Charlie. You thought I couldn't ... but up you, bastard.'

And maybe that's *why* I've done it. Maybe that's the *real* reason. To match him, man-for-man. To measure *my* indestructibility against *his*. Could be ... we sometimes have some damn funny reasons for doing damn funny things.

I crawl, unsteadily, across the tilting, swaying floor and collapse with my back against the wall, alongside the fire-place.

How long?

You tell *me*. How long did it take me to sculpture-work my wrist back into something resemblant of a wrist? How long have I sat here, alongside the fire, playing tag with unconsciousness? How long has it taken to live through this long and lousy day? A million years? ... I wouldn't argue.

For the moment, I am tired.

Too tired to answer damn-fool questions.

The come-to was gradual, but I am now back in working-order ... give or take a certain amount of exaggeration. The wrist is well padded with what was left of the sleeve-lining, and is bandaged as tightly as possible. I can even move my fingers. Stiffly, and painfully. But I can move them ... which means the bones are still intact and that, given time, the hand will return to normal.

It is nosh-time. Egon Ronay mightn't approve, but the chances are he's never cooked a meal—much less eaten one—in surroundings like these. Soup, followed by bacon and scrambled eggs, followed by hot, strong tea ... with biscuits all the way. Not West End fare but, for an empty stomach, food fit for the gods. I prepared the meal, and am pleasantly surprised to find that, with a tight wrist-bandage above bags of packing, my left hand can, at least, help my right. I wouldn't yet like to play Chopin with it ... but it isn't quite useless.

I do the thing right.

I bank the fire. I set the table—two places—and fill and light the Tilley as competition to the oncoming gloom of one more dusk.

Then, when everything's ready, I pick up the twelve-bore. I load both breeches and slip two new cartridges into my trouser pocket.

Then, I go into the scullery.

Charlie looks as tough as ever. The left side of his face has decided which colour it prefers—a very fetching mixture of blue, green and mauve—and his left eye is still merely a slit, surrounded by swollen flesh. Other than that, he seems okay. The cold (or so it seems) hasn't even touched him, and he is still married to the water pipe.

I rest the twin barrels of the shotgun in the crook of my left arm, move the safety-catch to 'off' and thumb back the hammers. I line the barrels onto his chest, curl the first and second fingers of my right hand around the triggers, and squeeze.

A shaved second before the hammers fall, I tilt the gun. The scullery shudders with the noise of the twin blasts, and another hole appears in the rear door of the farm-house.

It shakes him ... even Charlie.

'What the hell!' he gasps, and ducks to one side.

'Checking,' I murmur. 'That it still works. That you still remember what it can do.' I smile at him, and add, 'And,

137

Charlie, you were *yards* too late. You didn't dodge 'em.
If I'd kept its barrels trained, you'd be cat's meat.'

He takes a deep breath, and growls, 'What are you
proving this time, Cameron?'

'Just checking,' I repeat.

I break the gun and the spent cartridges are ejected
and fall to the floor of the scullery. I balance the gun in
the crook of my arm, fish fresh cartridges from my pocket
and re-load. Once more, I move the safety-catch to 'off'.
Once more I thumb back the hammers.

Then I reach into the pocket once more with my right
hand, take out the key to the handcuffs and toss it onto
the flagstones ... just out of his reach.

My fingers are on the triggers, and the gun is lined up
on him, as I kick the key towards him.

I say, 'Use it, Charlie.'

He doesn't move.

'Use it,' I repeat.

'You think I'm crazy?'

'Why not?' I mock. 'Have you fallen in love with that
length of water pipe?'

'If I touch that bloody key...'

'Nothing,' I assure him.

'If I unlock these cuffs...'

'Nothing.'

'You're a madman, Cameron.' For the first time, I see
something like apprehension in his eyes. 'You're looking
for an excuse. That's all. You're...'

'I'm hungry. I want company for dinner.'

'No! You're looking for an excuse...'

'If you're right,' I say, flatly. 'If I'm mad, why don't
I just blast you ... *then* unlock one of the cuffs.'

He considers the logic of what I've said.

'What's to stop me?' I taunt. 'Who'd know?'

Slowly—never taking his eye from the fingers which nurse the two triggers—he leans forward and picks up the key.

'Go ahead,' I encourage. 'There's food in the other room. Food, and good conversation. What more do you want?'

He holds the key, and calls, 'Hey! You in there...'

'He's asleep,' I lie. 'Fast asleep. He can't hear you.'

'He'll know.'

I shrug.

'He'll guess. Anything funny, and he'll guess.'

'So, what the hell scares you?'

'No ... I'm not scared, Cameron.' The pitch of his voice makes a mockery of the words. 'I'm not scared of *you*, Cameron. That'll be the day.'

I smile, and say, 'Unlock the cuff from the pipe, Charlie. The grub's getting cold.'

He hesitates—for maybe half-a-dozen heart beats—then, slowly, he uses the key and unhitches himself from the pipe.

'On your feet,' I order.

He hauls himself upright, and I watch the movement of every muscle.

I nod, and he walks into the main room. Stiffly ... as if he has cramp in his legs. And the chances are he *has* cramp in his legs.

'On the bed,' I say. 'Sit on the bed. Hook yourself to the bed-iron, then throw the key towards me.'

He lowers himself onto the edge of the bed, laces the handcuff to the angle iron, under the palliasse, then lobs the key in my direction. He glances at the face of the D.I. and almost says something.

Before he can speak, I snap, 'Now, stand up, Charlie.

Stand up, and shift the bed a little ... just to be sure you *have* turned the key.'

'Look—what the...'

'Up!' I encourage him with a movement of the twelve-bore.

He stands up, jerks his right hand, and the bed leaves the floor a fraction of an inch. It thumps back into position, and I'm satisfied. The bed is now an extension of his right hand.

Once more he glances at the thing under the blankets.

Once more I beat him to the punch, and speak first.

I say, 'Don't worry, Charlie. You won't disturb him.' I grin and add, 'Nobody's going to disturb him again.'

'You mean he's—he's ...?'

'Uhuh.' I nod, and keep grinning. 'We'll have a whip round for a wreath ... later.'

He lets out a soft, 'Oh!' and lowers himself slowly onto the edge of the bed.

I lean the shotgun against a wall. Using my thighs, I shunt the table across the flagstones, until it is in a comfortable position for him to eat. I position a chair. I pick up the shotgun, settle myself in the chair, lean the shotgun against the chair's back, and within quick and easy reach, and watch him from across the length of the table.

I say, 'Well?'

'I haven't figured it out, yet,' he says, slowly.

The pan of soup is on the table. The plates are in position. I lean across and pour soup into his plate, first. Then I pour soup into my own plate. I measure it carefully; we each get half.

I nod at the opened packet of crackers.

I say, 'Biscuits, Charlie. Help yourself.'

'What's happening, Cameron?' he asks, suspiciously.

'Biscuits,' I repeat. 'We're eating, Charlie. What else? We're hungry—both of us ... so, we're eating.'

Together we reach for the crackers. Together we each take a couple. Together we pick up our spoons and start on the soup. Twins—Siamese twins—that's what we are ... that's why we work in such harmony.

We sip and chew, as we talk.

'He's dead, Charlie.'

'So you say.'

'Feel him ... he's dead.'

'I'll take your word.'

'Dead ... and you killed him.'

'He *died*. There's a difference.'

'Not from a broken neck.'

'No ... not from a broken neck.'

'Nor from pneumonia.'

'Or from pneumonia.'

'From gunshot wounds, Charlie ... and you pulled the trigger.'

He moves his shoulders, and slurps his soup.

I say, 'You knew he was a cop, Charlie.'

'Yeah.'

'He identified himself ... shouted, when he knocked on the door.'

'Maybe I didn't hear him.'

'You heard him,' I chuckle.

'I can sometimes be very deaf.'

'You heard him ... I can give that evidence.'

'Is that a fact?'

'I was there. You *heard* him, Charlie.'

'That's your story.'

'Then, you bleated.'

'That's your story,' he repeats.

141

I smile along the table at him. Watch him wolf the soup and crackers, and know he's every bit as hungry as I am. I smile along the table at him ... and know I *have* him.

He's mine!

I can play with him as long as I like. Any game I like. Any rules I care to invent. I have waited a long time for this moment ... such a long, long time. I've prayed for it. Worked for it. Hoped for it. You name it—that's what I've done ... for this beautiful exquisite moment.

I murmur, 'You've blown it, Charlie.'

'Think so?'

'This time—you've blown it ... you've killed a very fancy policeman.'

'Maybe.'

'A New Scotland Yard detective inspector.'

'Knock it off, Cameron. You're getting nowhere.'

'They'll build a granite wall around you, Charlie. Then, they'll forget you're even around.'

'*If.*'

'Oh, I can give evidence, Charlie.' I treat him to a knowing, and very confident, smile. 'Against animals like you, I can give evidence ... all the evidence anybody could ever ask for.'

'The good old "verbals",' he sneers.

'And more. Much more.'

'Cooked evidence?' He looks interested. Mildly interested ... and a little worried.

'Your word, against mine,' I say, softly.

'About what?'

'Finish your soup, Charlie. The eggs and bacon are getting cold.'

'About *what?*' he insists.

142

I chuckle, quietly. Gently. At the secret thoughts tumbling around under the dome of my skull.

I say, 'Finish your soup, Charlie. Don't spoil a good meal by worrying ... it's bad for the indigestion.'

'You would, too,' he breathes.

'Oh, my word, yes.'

'Any bloody thing.'

'You name it.'

'Why?'

'Finish your soup, Charlie.'

'What the hell have *I* done?'

I push my empty plate to one side, and reach for the shotgun. I line the barrels along the top of the table, straight at his middle. The safety-catch is still at 'off'. The hammers are still cocked.

I hold the barrels steady with my left forearm, touch the triggers with the fingers of my right hand and, in a hard, cold, voice, say, 'That's an order, Charlie. Finish your soup. You live ... just as long as you do everything I say. Everything!'

He blinks his good eye, swallows, takes a deep breath, then croaks, 'Sure, Cameron. Sure ... anything.'

He finishes his soup. Every last drop.

We have eaten. I have shifted the table to the back of the room. We are now enjoying a quiet, friendly chat; smoking cigarettes; Charlie sitting on the edge of the bed, and I with my shoulder-blades resting against the wall, opposite him, and my legs stretched out and crossed in front of a good fire. The flagstones aren't particularly hard. Indeed, I hardly feel them; they are almost comfortable.

Nor is my wrist troubling me over-much. It's still there;

a little heavy and a little awkward, but without the ocean of pain it once held. What pain is left amounts to nothing. A thing of comparison ... a miniature, lost within the umpteen massive landscapes, seascapes and cloudscapes of pain which I have humped around for years. For more than fifteen years. I can, therefore, take a little more pain. I can tolerate a mere wristful of pain, for God's sake. A wristful ... a mere pinprick to add to the yawning chasm with which I have lived for the last fifteen years.

Comparisons ...

That's what it boils down to, and a wrist is nothing.

I say, 'Tell me about yourself, Charlie.'

'You already know.' The rusty-hinge voice sounds a mite unsure. A mite less cocky than it was a few hours ago. 'I've already told you about the act—The Goodwin Troup —what more do you ...?'

'After that,' I say. 'There's five years, between. Five years ago. What about those five years?'

'You're asking me to condemn myself. You're asking me to...'

'I'm asking you to talk, Charlie. That's all,' I say, dreamily. I reach a hand towards the shotgun, which is propped against the wall, alongside me. 'Conversation, Charlie. That's all I want. The lost art. To chat to each other. To share secrets. They're safe. They won't be used against you. Just talk, Charlie ... that's all.'

He looks at me, oddly—as oddly, and with as much curiosity, as he can, with one eye—then says, 'Cameron, are you ...?'

'Tell me about yourself, Charlie.'

The shotgun is levelled, cocked and ready.

'Sure.' He nods, eagerly. 'Sure ... what is it you want to know?'

'After the circus,' I say. 'We've heard about the circus. I know what happened *before* the circus. We're interested in what happened *after*. After the circus, Charlie ... that's what we want to hear about.'

He moistens his drying lips, glances up the bed, at the D.I., then talks.

After a flying act, what next? What *isn't* an anti-climax?
 What can equal it?
 Nothing!
 Charlie toyed with the idea of an animal act; a cat act. Tigers ... the *real* monarchs of the cat-world. Two things stopped him. The expense; tigers might *look* like over-grown kittens, but they're a damn sight more pricey to buy and a damn sight more pricey to keep. And the knack; the sheer, can't-be-taught know-how of facing a cageful of striped killers, and dominating them.

Circus folk help each other. They tried to help Charlie.

The Circus Knie and the Chipperfield family did what they could. They listened, and appreciated his ambition. They gave him a try-out ... then, they each told the truth. He lacked it. He had the courage—he had the raw nerve ... but he lacked that something which, when the cats felt mean, would save his life.

Half a dozen times, he walked into the cage ... alone.

And, half a dozen times, the cats became restless. They knew this stranger wasn't their master, and never would be. Their instinct told them. Any time—any time they liked, at rehearsal or under the spots—they could have him. They could take him. They could open his guts, or chew an arm off, before an attendant had time to rod them clear.

The Knie people and the Chipperfield family told him.

'Take cats. Tigers. Build up an act, if you must. But we won't back you. We'll teach you—as much as anybody can teach you—but we won't finance you. There's a reason, and it's an honest reason. You won't last. You'll be mauled. If not while you're training them, in the first season. It's happened before ... too many times. You lack the magic, Goodwin. You lack the mastery. Be told, friend—for your own sake, take advice—forget the big cats ... look around for another catcher.'

Such good advice ... and so easy.

So obvious.

'Look around for another catcher.'

Like all you have to do is whistle, and a Charles Clarke comes running; Charles Clarke, the man who caught his brother Ernest in a *quadruple* back somersault, in practice, one day in Mexico City. Like there is a Lee Strath Marilees hanging around at every street corner; Lee Strath Marilees, of 'The Flying Marilees' who, also in Mexico—in Durango —in 1962, first caught Tony Steele, in a triple-and-a-half back somersault, *which was part of the act.*

They meant well, when they said, 'Look around for another catcher', but they also knew they were giving near-impossible advice. For a catcher is like a gold nugget in a council tip. As rare as *that.* And, supposing Charlie had found another catcher ... what then? From the start-line ... that's what.

It would have meant a completely new act. At least a year of hard practice—at *least* a year ... not merely to forget the old tricks, and learn the new, but to get the 'feel' of the strange hands reaching out from the catching bar.

From king to nothing.

When the Pole crossed himself, then turned and walked

away from the ring, Charlie Goodwin was dethroned ...
but good!

I flip what is left of my cigarette into the hearth, and
say, 'Then what?'

'I bummed around.'

'Doing what?'

'Wasting time.'

'Circus?'

'Good God, no.'

'No?' I put on a look of surprise.

'Once a flyer, nothing else.'

'Nothing less than tigers.'

'Uhuh.' He nods, and takes a last draw at his cigarette,
before throwing it onto the hearth, alongside mine.

It's night, outside, by this time. The wind has risen
a little. Not a howler—not like it was yesterday—but
enough to clear the mist. I can hear it, beyond the stone
walls of the farmhouse; below the roar of deep waters
which fills my head.

It could freeze, tonight. It could very easily freeze ...
indeed, maybe it's already touching freezing-point, outside. I wouldn't be too surprised. The fire has burned a little
low, and there is a touch of cold in the room. Not enough
to worry about ... just a touch.

I grin at him, and say, 'Then what?'

'What?'

'Your life, Charlie. After the circus. The last five years
... we're interested.'

He frowns, and says, 'Look—what the hell are you ...?'

'I'm not anxious to kill you, Charlie.' I move a hand
towards the shotgun. 'I don't *want* to kill you.' I smile as
I speak and, in my mind, I add the word 'yet'.

147

'I bummed around,' he says, hurriedly. 'I've already said. I wasted time. Looking for another catcher. Wondering about the cat-act. In the circus ... but *not* in the circus. It's hard to explain.'

'Try.'

'Okay—okay ... but, don't blame me if it's boring.'

Nothing Charlie Goodwin ever did was boring ... except to himself. He bored readily, because he was an all-action man. He couldn't sit still. He wasn't capable of making life a single, comfortable groove. He needed movement. He needed excitement. He needed *people* ... in particular, he needed people he could shove around, and who enjoyed being shoved around by Charlie Goodwin. People he could dominate. People who were a little scared of him, and who treated him as their natural leader—their superior—the personification of their own much-improved alter ego.

As a flyer, that was okay. His needs were catered for. His wasn't the best troup in the world—but he made damn sure it was always the top act in whichever ring they played ... and that was good enough.

As an ex-flyer, he was a little like an ex-dictator. An ex-superintendent of police. An ex-army general. An ex-*anything*.

He was granted passing courtesy, but old, and hidden, enmities edged their way into the open and showed themselves. Jealousies and envies were no longer kept under wraps ... and some of them had a lot of leeway to make up.

The circus world is like every other world. It pays homage to the best ... but only while the best *is* the best. Thereafter, it is studiously polite. The second-best it tolerates, then when the second-best isn't even *second-best*, the brush-off technique takes over.

From loving the ring people, Charlie gradually came to scorn them.

He expanded his circle of 'friends'. Circus. General show-biz. Night-clubs. Strip-joints. Gambling-spots. The blanket term 'entertainment' included some very shady characters, and Charlie met, and befriended, some of these characters.

From then on, the slide down gathered momentum.

He could drive well. He was the 'wheel man' in a trio of hick-town hold-ups. On the last of the three, he out-drove and out-foxed a pursuing squad car ... and that earned him a name for cool nerve and reliability.

From 'wheel man' he became 'enforcer'. The Protection Racket is built upon terror, and men who can instil terror; men who don't give a damn about being identified; men who have confidence in their own muscle—in their own ruthlessness ... whose safety rests upon the knowledge that those who *can* identify *daren't* identify.

It was nice, while it lasted. Lucrative. Exciting. Non-boring. But he wasn't the boss-man. He *took* orders ... and Charlie Goodwin wasn't going to be satisfied until he *gave* orders.

A gang—some sort of personal mob—was the only answer. Nothing big ... not for starters. Nothing of a size likely to worry the well-established 'firms'. A handful of picked men—no more than six—all disciplined, and trained to obey orders.

In effect, another 'Goodwin Troup' ... but, this time, not for the high trapeze.

*   *   *

'Picked men,' I sneer. 'Disciplined men. Trained to obey orders.'

'Second-best,' says Charlie, flatly. 'The best all belonged ... they weren't available.'

'Didn't you figure?' I chuckled at his naïvety.

'They were getting better.'

'Is that a fact?'

'The bank job wasn't the first.'

'No?'

'We'd bad luck ... that's all.'

'How many jobs?' I ask.

'Cameron.' He shakes his head. 'You don't *ask* those sort of questions.'

'*I* do.'

'Yeah ... you always were an optimist.'

Optimist! *Me*, an optimist ... oh, my Christ! You name it; if it's capable of being screwed I'm the boy to screw it. Career, marriage, parenthood, life ... the lot. I can't even pull a straightforward pinch, without isolating myself in a Tops farmhouse; without wandering around, lost, in the mist; without damn near tearing my hand off. Friend —I ask you ... what the hell have *I* to be optimistic about?

Once upon a time, maybe. Before life upped and kicked my teeth out, one at a time. When I was single. When I was happy. Twenty years back, when the world was two decades younger than it is today, and two decades less sour-tasting ... maybe then. Maybe *then*, I was crazy enough to believe in a little thing called optimism.

Today!

Oh, Jesus, link the name of Ray Cameron with even a whiff of optimism, and make a joke. Make the biggest joke since Nixon raised surprised eyebrows at the name 'Watergate' ... and that *brand* of joke. Sick and private. Non-funny and very personal.

I laugh, quietly, to myself at this very private—very non-funny—joke.

Charlie watches, with a puzzled expression wrinkling his bruised and swollen face.

'Ever get round to marrying, Charlie?' I ask.

'No.'

'No ... *you* wouldn't.'

'What's that mean?'

'You've more sense. You're too cunning.'

'What's eating you, Cameron?' asks Charlie, gently.

'Eating me?'

'Yeah—eating you ... what the hell's *wrong* with you, Cameron?'

'I asked a question, that's all. I made an observation, Charlie ... no more than that. That you're too damn cunning ever to get married.'

'All right.' Charlie takes a deep breath, then repeats, 'All *right*. You've made the observation. Fine. So, what? Where's the reason for all the hilarity?'

'Hilarity?' I don't follow his thought process.

'The laughter?'

'Was I *laughing*?'

'Yeah,' he sighs. 'You were laughing. You were having funnies, all by yourself.'

'Oh ... *that*?'

'Yeah. That.'

I say, 'Private, Charlie. Private ... even from you. A very private joke. You wouldn't get it. You wouldn't see the point ... never having been married.'

'What the hell ...?'

'*I* got married.'

'Eh?'

'I married,' I repeat, dreamily. 'A nice girl. A good woman. A good wife. We even had a kid—a son ... so, that makes me a father, Charlie.'

'Is that funny? Is that unusual?'

'No-o,' I concede, reluctantly. 'What makes it funny is that he was a nutter ... the kid, I mean. Sub-normal. That's the official term. His brain was so much scrambled egg.'

'I'm—er—I'm sorry. I didn't ...'

'He died.'

'Oh!'

'And that turned *her* brain.'

He chews his lip, for a moment, then mutters, 'I'm sorry, Cameron. I know—it doesn't mean much ... me being sorry. But I am. That's rough, on any man.'

'Rough,' I agree, in a toneless voice. 'No bastard knows *how* rough. I loved that kid—I loved 'em both, Charlie ... nobody knows *how* rough.'

'We—er—we need to see a doctor, honey,' I say, hesitantly.

'Why?'

She asks the question, but she knows the answer. She must know the answer. The question is a blind—a tissue-thin blind—from which she tries to hide from the truth.

I put all the love I'm capable of into my voice, when I say, 'Honey, he should be doing things by this time. He should be house-trained. He should be taking notice. He should be talking ... just a few words.'

'He's a little slow, that's all. A slow starter.'

'Honey, he's ...'

152

'*A slow starter! Lots of people are slow starters. I don't want a genius for a son.*'

I close my eyes, helplessly, and breathe, '*Judas Christ, honey.*'

'*Don't blaspheme, Ray. Blaspheming won't help him.*'

It's an admission ... of a sort. That the kid needs *help*. It's a peep-hole in the blind. Something. The first part-acceptance of what we both know.

I work to tear the blind aside ... but with as little hurt as possible.

I lean forward in the chair, and say, '*Honey, I love him. I don't have to tell you. I love him, as much as you do. I love you both.*'

'*There's nothing* wrong *with him!*'

I look at the kid; at the eyes, filled with innocent wonder, but no curiosity; at the mouth, with its never-ending thread of spittle running from one corner; at the head, which I know—which she knows—lacks its full quota of gear-wheels. All this I see, and all that I see tears at my guts like a band-saw. I love the kid ... despite what the hell's wrong with the poor little bastard, I love him. I love his mother ... the gentlest creature ever to draw God's air into her lungs.

And yet ...

At this moment, she loathes me. She is fighting, like a wild-cat, in defence of her injured kitten. She won't be-lieve, because she doesn't want to believe. She spits the truth back at me and, for the moment, she loathes me.

I plead, '*Honey, if he had chicken pox. Measles. A broken arm. You'd do something. We'd both do all we could. We'd call in the experts. The medics. We'd need help ... we'd go for help.*'

'*There's nothing* wrong *with him!*'

'*It's the same thing, honey. No different. We can't help him. We can love him—okay, we* do *love him ... but we can't* help *him. We don't know how.*'

'*No! I'll not let you ...*'

'*Not me, honey. Not just me. You, too ... you, a damn sight more than me. He's dragging the life out of you. He doesn't mean to—because he doesn't know ... if he knew, he wouldn't want it. But he's making you old, before your time. He's making you ...*'

'*I'm not stopping you.*' It comes as a snarl. As a spitting defiance.

'*What?*' If she means what I think she means, she's crazy.

'*Go find a younger woman—some street-corner tart—if that's what you want. I'm not stopping you.*'

'*God damn it! That's not what I said ... and you know it.*' I am suddenly very angry. I, who was going to be so gentle—so considerate, in easing her towards an acceptance of the truth—blow my top, and become very nasty. Very vicious. Very hurtful. I bawl, '*Face facts ... for Christ's sake. He's not just "backward". He's not just a "slow starter". He's a dummy. And you won't accept it and, because you won't accept it, he's draining the juice out of you. You're a young woman, for Christ's sake. You're not a hag ... yet. But that's what he's making you. And you soon will be, unless we stop all this stupidity.*'

'*All right ... go find yourself somebody who isn't a hag.*'

'*Don't twist my words, girl. Don't ...*'

'*Go find somebody who uses your sort of language.*'

'*For Christ's sake. What the hell have I ...*'

'*Just leave me alone.*'

'*The kid. He's ...*'

'*He's* normal!'

'*The hell he's normal. He's a dummy. We need help with him.*'

'*There's nothing* wrong *with him.*'

'*You mad bitch. Can't you see?* Won't *you see? We're being smashed to hell, because we've a kid who's...*'

She hugs the kid closer, and screams, 'Leave me alone! Leave me alone! *Go out and find a slut, if that's what you want. I don't care. I don't care, at all. Go out and find yourself a slut ... but, LEAVE ME ALONE!*'

'I did, too,' I mumble.

'Eh?' Charlie frowns non-understanding.

'A slag.'

'What about slags?'

'I got one.'

'Your wife? She was a slag? I thought you said she was...'

'Charlie, why don't you listen?' I plead.

'Say something, and I'll listen.'

He says, 'Your wife—your kid ... you were telling me about them. Then slags came into it. The gist escapes me. That's all.'

'I went out with a slag ... that's all,' I sigh.

'Yeah—well ... don't we all?'

'A cheap, pay-by-the-minute shag-session.'

He murmurs, 'Come down to earth, Cameron.'

'Charlie,' I explain, 'you can't get more "earthy" than a quick-time bout on a whore's bed. It doesn't help. It doesn't help one little bit.'

'Sometimes,' he says, quietly.

'You dumb bastard, Charlie!' I explode. 'How the hell can it help? Shafting some glossy-arsed tart ... how the hell can *that* help, when you've a kid who's a nutter and a wife who doesn't want to know?'

'Okay ... it doesn't help,' he soothes.

The rage leaves me, as quickly as it arrived.

I mumble, 'You should listen, Charlie. Listen. Y'know ... learn a few things.'

'Sure.'

'There's a lot to tell you, Charlie. We've got all the time in the world ... and I have one hell of a lot to tell you.'

CHAPTER ELEVEN

'Cameron! Cameron! Hey, Cameron!'

I swing back, from wherever I've been, and Charlie's face joins Charlie's voice. His bashed-up face has a troubled look, and he is on his feet—still linked to the bed—trying to drag the bed, and its occupant across the room.

I blink myself back to reality, and snarl, 'Don't get ambitious, Charlie.'

I grab for the shotgun, and he stops his tug-of-war and stands very still.

'You flaked out,' he growls.

'I dropped off. I've had a heavy day.'

I grip the gun round the stock, and raise my left hand to hold the barrels ... but the left hand won't come. It stays put, on the stone floor, alongside my rump. I glance down at it, and try to figure things out.

The hell I 'dropped off' ... for some reason, I just stopped being around. And the reason doesn't come readily. That damn hand—the wrist, tied tighter than a mummy's—doesn't hurt any more. Doesn't hurt, doesn't throb, doesn't *anything*. It just isn't there. No feeling ... just weight. Like a ton of lead, lashed to my left shoulder and holding me in place.

I wedge the stock of the shotgun against the angle of the wall and floor, tilt the barrels till they point where I want them to point, and say, 'Sit down, Charlie. Don't try anything.'

He lowers himself onto the edge of the bed.

We watch each other for a few moments. Playing bluff against bluff; expression against expression. He leads with something which might be mistaken for concern, I follow with a look of assured contempt. Mock-worry is met with sneering confidence. The game is a kid's game—pulling faces at each other ... but the twelve-bore makes it a very adult version.

The fire is low, and the cold from the outside night is creeping through hidden cracks and taking over. The Tilley isn't as bright as it should be—the mantle should be white, but it is a bright yellow—and it needs a few strokes on the pump to bring it up to full glow.

'How long?' I ask, flatly.

'What?'

'Have I been asleep?'

'Thirty minutes—thereabouts ... but not asleep.'

'I just dozed off, Charlie,' I insist.

He shakes his head, and says, 'Cameron, you went under. I know sleep, when I see it.'

'For thirty minutes?' Disbelief is in my voice.

'Uhuh.' He nods.

'And you didn't make a play?'

'With a bed under my arm?' His mouth twists into a sardonic smile.

'If it was more than sleep.'

'Let's say I had to be sure.'

'Okay ... let's say you had to be sure.'

'Cameron...' He pauses then, in a sombre voice, says, 'What's boiling up inside you is dynamite. What it is, I don't know ... or why. But it's more than law. More than fuzz. It's a personal thing.'

'Between us two?' I taunt.

'I dunno. I've never met it, before. Between you and *people* like me ... maybe that.'

'I've felt collars, before today.'

'This way?'

'I have a reputation ... so they tell me.'

'You're not alone, Cameron.'

'I know.'

'You're unique.'

I grin up at him, then raise the barrels of the shotgun and lean it back against the wall.

The fire needs more fuel. The lamp needs more pressure. I have to drag myself upright.

I make it, too!

Charlie watches. He sees a man with the grin of a loon plastered across his face; a man who is working to hide all the left-handed threading which has suddenly built up inside. The arm ... useless, and heavy enough to drop the left shoulder out of line. The staggers ... like I've been mixing the shorts too wildly, and am more than a little gassed.

I try not to let it show. I try to keep the knee-joints under control. I try to keep things in focus. I try to counter the bent-forward shuffle.

I feed logs and coal to the fire. I hold the Tilley steady with the weight of my left arm, and pump more life into the flame. I return to my place, alongside the gun, rest my shoulder blades against the wall and let my legs bend. I slide down the wall ... and it is like taking time off to rest, after a brisk walk up a mountain. Say, Everest!

One-handed, I light a cigarette and almost wish I hadn't. The trickle of smoke from the tip exaggerates the shakes.

'Bad?' asks Charlie.

'I am unique, Charlie,' I croak. 'You made the observation. Hope that's *all* I am ... because, if I'm going, I send you before I set off.'

He nods perfect understanding.

I smoke awhile. I hold a no-holds-barred wrestling match with myself, inside. I hook a full Nelson onto my thinking equipment, force it into submission, and return to normal —sorry! ... to *near*-normal.

In a tired voice, I say, 'I've been thinking, Charlie.'

He waits, expectantly.

'That second Goodwin Troup,' I murmur. 'The one that didn't fly.'

'What about it?'

'You were boss-man, Charlie.'

'It's one admission I've made.'

'And ten thousand left that bank, after the raid.'

'That's what the papers say.'

'That's what *happened*, Charlie. My info comes from crime sheets ... not yellow rags.'

'So?'

'Ten thousand crispies ... and you're the boss-man,' I smile.

'If you say so, Cameron.' He tries to sound bored, but the hell he's bored ... he's *worried*.

'They're around,' I say.

His good eye narrows, slightly.

I nod towards the cupboard and, at the same time, reach for the gun.

I say, 'Off your rump, Charlie. I need fresh cartridges ... and I think you can just about make it.'

'Why the hell should I? I'd be a damn fool...'

'You'll be a *dead* fool, if you don't!'

'I dunno what...'

'Charlie,' I drone, as I line up the barrels. 'I don't give one tiny damn. Believe me. You want your guts sprayed across that wall—okay ... will do. I'll not ask you to reach those cartridges twice. I'll use the two I've already got.'

He believes me. He'd *better* believe me. He stands up from the bed and, by kneeling down and stretching both arms, he catches his fingers around the box of cartridges, pulls it closer, then shoves it across the floor to where I'm sitting. And why not? He isn't dumb. He isn't a coward. He's very wise. He wants to live ... as long as possible.

He returns to the edge of the bed and as he sits down he moves the blanket, and the face of the dead D.I. peeks out ... as if the New Scotland Yard boyo is playing Peeping Tom on a show, of which he is not a part.

I rest the gun across my knees, long enough for me to grab a handful of bang-bang tubes and drop them on the floor, alongside my good hand. I pick up the shotgun, position it with the butt wedged between wall and floor and estimate the angle of the barrels.

I squeeze both triggers.

That twin-sized explosion does a lot of things, all at the same time. It bucks the gun a little. It sends about two-and-a-half ounces of buckshot ripping across the room, low enough to stir the breeze and ruffle Charlie's hair. It gouges plaster out of ceiling and wall, and sprays a white shower over Charlie and the bed. It sends Charlie tumbling backward, awkwardly because of his cuffed hand, and across the corpse ... a million miles too late to have ducked the blast. It makes the whole damn room quiver with noise, makes the flames in the hearth curtsey as they receive the backlash ... and makes my skull vibrate, like a Chinese gong which has just been kicked by an elephant.

I whisper, 'Jesus!' and almost drop the gun to grab my head.

Instead, I haul myself onto a tighter rein, break the breech and, as the spent cartridges fly, replace them with new ones.

'Up, Charlie,' I say, hoarsely. 'When I want to take your head off, I won't miss.'

As he slowly pushes himself upright, he snarls, 'You have rocks between the ears, Cameron.'

'Maybe.'

'You've flipped to the B-side.'

'Wassat?' I can't hear too well, for the surf pounding away under my thatch.

'You're bloody mad!'

'Uhuh ... could be.'

I nod ... and wish I hadn't. The sea of curd inside my head slops around, and past foams in with present and spumes my mind with memories ...

... He is already dead. I don't need medical verification.

The tyre bounced a path across his tiny chest ... and that did it.

He hangs there, cradled in my arms, with his neck loose and his head flopping and, from a corner of his mouth, a trickle of blood is already working a path towards one of his eyes ...

... 'Hey, Cameron. Snap out of it. C'mon—snap out of it!'

'Wassat?'

'Back, man. To the land of the living. Don't go stiff on me, Cameron. Not you, too. Don't make it *two* coppers.'

A frog-voice mumbles, 'You getting worried, Charlie?'

'Yeah ... I'm getting worried.'

'Great.'

'What the hell's great? What the hell sort of ...?'

'I licked you, Charlie.'

'Okay—okay ... you've licked me. I just don't want two stiffs around. They wouldn't believe me. They'd crucify me, Cameron. You know that ... they'd crucify me.'

'You wouldn't like that, Charlie. You wouldn't enjoy it...'

...'*You're not going to enjoy it, Ray.*'

'*I've seen bodies before.*'

'*It's—er—y'know ...*'

'*Necessary. I know.*'

'*Coroners. Inquests. It's...*'

'*It's necessary, mate. Don't bugger about making empty excuses for what's necessary.*'

'*No—I wasn't—but...*'

'*Just pull the sheet down. Let me identify him. Then, let's get out of here.*'

'*I know, Ray. Mortuaries. They give me the creeps. They're...*'

'*They're something else that's necessary.*'

'*I—er—I suppose.*'

'*Get on with it. Let's get out of here.*'

'*Of course, Ray. When you're ready.*'

'*I'm ready, now. I've been ready...*'

'... get out of here, Ray.'

'Whaaa...'

'For Christ's sake, grab yourself, Cameron. Grab yourself, Ray.'

'Ray?' I blink the past out of my mind, and come back

to the stone-flagged floor of a farmhouse, on the Tops. I squint up at him, and slur, 'You called me Ray? Why the sudden friendship?'

'It's not sudden.' There's urgency in his tone. 'It's been there a lifetime, pal. Remember? The inseparables ... remember?'

'I remember,' I mutter. 'Too damn well, I remember. You, riding out on top of a ...'

'Forget that. Forget that part.' I can hear his breathing. Fast and a little heavy. He says, 'Listen—listen, Ray ... I think I can reach the whisky. I'm going to get up from the bed ... okay?'

'No tricks.' I curl my hand around the stock of the shot-gun. 'No tricks, Charlie.'

'I swear.'

'Just remember ... that's all.'

'I want you with me, Ray. Can't you understand? I want you *with* me ... I think the whisky might help.'

'Just be careful ... that's all.'

'Okay.'

I watch him, and make-believe I can see him. I *can* see him ... but the vision is as if I'm watching through pebbled glass. I can see the form. I can see the shape. I can see the movement. I can see the blur of colour. The details? ... I *pretend* the details. He could be anybody, doing just about anything, but I know damn well who he is and I think I know what he's doing.

I peer through the pebbled glass, and follow the moving form with the twelve-bore barrels.

Something knocks against my knee, and he says, 'A deep swig, Ray. Deep, and hard ... it'll help.'

'Back to the bed, Charlie.'

'Sure. Sure.'

The form moves, then stops. I give it a moment or two ... just to make sure.

He says, 'Okay, Ray. Take a swig. It'll help.'

I trust him—the hell I trust him! ... but what else? I position the shotgun across my knees, reach out and feel for the bottle. I hold the bottle tight, between my thighs, fumble around a little, then unscrew the cap and tip whisky down my throat.

What happens justifies every distillery pushing out hooch. It is excuse enough for every illegal still ever set up by a bootlegging booze-pedlar. Golden nectar—nothing less—gurgles down my throat, and liquid life begins to circulate through my body. The sea of turbulence, under my skull, quietens down considerably. Charlie zooms into vision; I see his smacked-around face, his stained clothes and his good eye ... an eye which wears a lot of worry and unease.

I grin at him, move the bottle in a tiny wave, and say, 'Hiya, Charlie.'

'Easy, pal.' The concern in his voice matches the worry in his eye.

'S'okay, Charlie.'

'Just don't rush things ... that's all.'

'S'okay. I'm back from the land of the zombies.'

He nods, as if half-convinced.

'S'okay, Charlie. I'm still running things.'

'Sure.' He glances at the bottle, and adds, 'I could enjoy the last half inch.'

'Who knows?' I cork the almost-empty bottle and position it, very carefully, alongside my right elbow. I curl my fingers around the gun, again, and say, 'Before the gremlins tried to take over. We were having a very interesting debate ... remember?'

'No. I dunno what...'

'Charlie!' I warn.

'Okay. Remind me.'

'Ten G. Ten thousand sweet little smackers.'

'Oh ... that?'

'That,' I agree. 'And where they are.'

'I wouldn't know.'

'Charlie,' I ask, with interest, 'you figure I've got all my wicks trimmed, at the moment?'

'Eh?'

'Any goof-ups, north of my eyebrows?'

'You've been hammered,' he foxes.

'Charlie!'

'Okay. You've been hammered ... badly. You've talked a little. Crazy talk.'

'Crazy talk?' I'm interested.

'About your kid—I think ... one of your kids.'

'I only ever had one kid, Charlie.'

'Okay ... *that* kid.'

'What about my kid?' For the time being, the fiscal talk can wait.

'I dunno.' He moves his shoulders.

'Come on, Charlie. What did I say?'

'About him being killed. About him being run over—something ... it didn't make too much sense.'

'Just that?'

'Cameron, I wasn't too interested.'

'No?' The hatred comes back with a rush; like a dam cracking, and all the millions of tons of water, and all the broken concrete, and all earth which has held it in position. It all comes—smashing, crashing, splintering, destroying ... and it's all hatred. More hatred than one man should

166

have to hold. I snarl, 'What did I say, Charlie? Just what did I *say*?'

'Just that.' His face twists into a look of worry. A very personal worry. He hesitates, then adds, 'The dummy— if you've only ever had one kid ... it must have been about the dummy.'

'Uhuh. He was a dummy. He couldn't think. He couldn't think ... not even enough not to empty his bowels, all over the place.' I glance at the dead D.I., and say, 'Like that one. Crazy.'

'Yeah ... you said.'

'And a car backed over him.'

'Rough.'

'He was playing in the drive, see ... and this car backed over him.'

'Rough,' repeats Charlie.

I mutter, 'Some accidents are bad. No good ones ... but some accidents are bad.'

'I know. I've seen accidents.'

'Not like this one, Charlie. Not as bad as this one. His own drive ... in the drive of his own home. Dammit, his own toy! His own teddy bear. He was playing with it, when the car backed over him.'

'I'm sorry, Cameron. I didn't know the kid, but ...'

'Sorry!' I explode. 'Jesus God, how does *that* help? You, being sorry. I was driving the bloody car. Me! I was the bastard behind the wheel—backing the car into the road ... *I was driving the bloody car.*'

'Judas Christ!' he breathes.

'And *you're* sorry.'

'It shouldn't happen,' he says, softly. 'It shouldn't happen to any man.'

I quieten a little, and say, 'I doubled the dummy stakes,

167

Charlie. Just like *that*. It sent his mother over the edge ...
I switched one dummy for another. That's nice ... eh?
That's poetic justice ... eh?'

'That,' says Charlie, solemnly, 'is a cow of a thing to
have to live with.'

'Yeah.'

'I'm sorry, Cameron ... I'm truly sorry.'

'Where did the "Ray" go?' I ask, harshly. 'All that
buddy-buddy bullshit ... where did *that* go?'

Very quietly—very sombrely—he says, 'We're cop and
robber, Cameron.'

'No ... cop and *murderer*.'

'Whatever ... not friends. Whatever we once were.'

'It's ancient history, Charlie,' I say, heavily.

'Just that. Nice to remember ... but ancient history.'

'And we were talking about money.'

'No.' He shakes his head. '*You* were talking about
money.'

'Ten thousand iron men,' I say, coldly. 'I want 'em
Goodwin. They're the price of your life—the *exact* price
... ten thousand notes. Get 'em!'

CHAPTER TWELVE

What choice has the creep? He can take the same medicine he fed to the D.I.—he can have his legs blasted off, below the knee-caps ... which is the medicine I offer, as a sure cure for a tight mouth. He can take two in the guts ... then I can wait here, until I build up enough steam to perform my own hunt-the-slipper routine.

So-o ... what the hell choice has the creep?

Because—y'see—I know Charlie. Charlie, and his 'Goodwin Troup' ... both of them. The führer ... that's Charlie. He hasn't changed; when a man's as cocksure of himself as Charlie is—as he always will be—he can be relied upon to do certain things. To trust *nobody*.

Ten thousand smackers found a new owner after that bank raid, and the name of that new owner has to be Charlie Goodwin. There hasn't been time for a share-out. Three of the others are already inside, anyway ... and they were damn near living on tick. So, that leaves Charlie and, where Charlie is, that's where the moolah is. *Here*—within reach—and now it's going to get another new owner ... or else!

I take my time, line the shotgun, bridge the hammers with my thumb and squeeze both triggers all the way back. The pressure of my thumb is the only thing holding the buckshot in the breech.

'Don't think I won't, Charlie,' I say, gently. 'Don't *ever* think I won't.'

169

'You'd be a killer, Cameron.' His voice has ragged edges. 'You'd be a murderer.'

'Speaking as an expert.' I glance at the tumbled corpse, on the bed.

'Yeah ... but you're a cop.'

'You can't do it, Charlie,' I assure him.

'Do what?'

'Talk me out of it. Don't try ... this thumb might get a little muscle-weary, if it holds these hammers too long.'

'You're a *cop*!'

That last word tells the whole story. That, hard as he is—hard as he's become—I've softened him. The old, old formula—the difference between a champ and a ring-legend ... he can dish out more than he can take. The difference between Charlie Goodwin and Ray Cameron; that Charlie Goodwin can soak up punishment to a very wide limit ... but that Ray Cameron *has* no limit!

I am not a vain man, but I feel a sense of pride. On my knees, I can *still* lick him. On my back, *I'm* still his equal ... and more than his equal.

This hand—this arm ... and he falls back on the last argument in the book.

I'm a cop.

From somewhere not far from the soles of my feet I drag up enough energy to put whiplash scorn into my voice.

I say, 'Charlie, boy, forget the "cop" tag. It won't stop me from blasting plate-sized holes through you. It takes a bastard to beat a bastard, Charlie. You're a bastard ... but I'm a bigger bastard. I've worked at it, for a long, long time. I've had practice. Any milk of human kindness I might have had turned into lemon juice, years ago.'

He stares, from his good eye, for a moment then, in a

flat, dead voice, says, 'You mean it. You really *mean* it.'

'Try me, Charlie.'

'Why?'

'No arguments. No explanations. If the money isn't available, that bed holds two stiffs. *Now*, Charlie.'

There is one last, empty hesitation, then he says, 'Upstairs ... in one of the bedrooms.'

'Front? Back?'

'Back ... some of the plaster's off the wall. There's a zip holdall. It's hidden under a pile of plaster, in one corner.'

'Ten thou?'

He nods, sourly.

I ease the hammers down, and take my fingers from the triggers.

I say, 'Congratulations. You've just bought your life, Charlie.'

In a voice, as sour as the nod, he says, 'Now, get it, Cameron. You clawing across this room—you climbing those stairs ... this I have to see.'

We-ell—maybe *he* couldn't ... but *I* can!

I do it on my knees, because it's safer that way. I don't fall too far, when I keel over. I do it on my knees, helped a little by my right hand, and dragging my left arm along for the ride. I take the dizziness with me, every inch of the way ... the coming-and-going roar of what the hell it is inside my skull.

I do it in short hops, on my knees. Pushing the shotgun and the Tilley ahead of me. Waiting, every few yards, until my eyes focus themselves again, then aiming for a point a few yards ahead. Timing it. Knowing that, every seven or eight shuffles, I'm going to flop sideways and sprawl, until the cool touch of the flagstones brings back the will to force another few shuffles behind me.

I detour the bed, and make for the scullery. I crawl the scullery and reach one corner, where the stairs begin. It is a journey to the end of the earth ... it takes me all of twenty minutes and, in those twenty minutes, I roll onto my side six (maybe seven) times.

But I make it.

I leave the shotgun at the foot of the stairs.

I take the stairs, step at a time. Lifting the Tilley ahead of me; placing it, with exaggerated care, before I drag myself up one more step. I take the steps on my arse—one at a time—with my back propped against the wall of the stairway. Sideways, with the weight of the useless, waterlogged arm trying to pull me back, into the scullery.

I don't flake out at each step—not at every step ... only at most of them. But I come to some sort of terms with the whirling darkness. I know when it's coming. I have half a second of semi-consciousness, before the lights dim and, in that half second, I tilt my body a little ... organising things, very carefully, in order that I flop to my right and *into* the steps. That way—with luck—I won't end back on the scullery floor ...' and I have *that* much luck.

Clever?

I think so ... I think it's one of the cleverest things I've ever done in my life.

And, if I don't turn to water, I'll make it.

If I don't turn to water. Sweat! Sweet Jesus, I'm leaking the damn stuff. It's like pushing a way up, through Niagara. Moisture splashes from my forehead; soaks my clothes, from the skin, out; makes my hand slippery, on the stone of the steps.

Niagara—just like Niagara—as crazy, and as impossible,

as Niagara ... and the roar of the tumbling torrent drowns all other noise.

I can't make it—*nobody* can make it ... but *I* do!

Another twenty minutes—maybe half an hour ... what the hell's time, anyway? A decade—a century—a million years ... and I'm in the front bedroom, sprawling on the muck-thick boards and panting for the return of some sort of life.

My legs are starting to shake, so the rest of it is crawl ... not even on my knees.

Crawl. Foot at a time. Pushing the Tilley ahead of me. Across the bedroom, and towards the door leading to the rear bedroom. Through mouse- and rat-droppings; through tiny heaps of pigeon shit; through dust and muck an inch thick. And, like a snail, I leave a crazy path of moisture behind me ... moisture, which is the sweat which still pours out of me.

Dignity? What, in hell's name, is dignity? Give a man enough hatred. Give him enough pain. Give him enough suffering—enough bitterness—enough hurt—and he'll crap all the dignity he ever possessed down the nearest john, and not even know he's parted. All he wants is revenge and, to get revenge, he'll haul himself backwards, through hell itself, by the balls.

I know what I say. I know the truth of it, and the truth of it is something I've come to accept ... something I still accept.

And, now, I'm proving that truth.

If I crawled through that front bedroom, foot at a time, I made good progress. I take the rear bedroom, inch at a time ... literally. I take it on my side, with my right hand reaching out to claw a way towards the dung-heap of old plaster stacked in one corner. I take it with my right cheek touching the floorboards; with filth and vermin-leavings building up and spilling into the corner of my mouth.

Dignity? Dignity, be damned! All I want is that money ... and, with it, a final pay-off.

I take the sweat with me. I take the noise with me. I take my numb, and useless, body with me. Because *I'm* going ... which means they, too, must go.

How long?

God knows.

How long before bleeding finger-nails have scratched a way through the plaster and uncovered the zipped-up holdall?

Again, God knows.

And then, the return journey.

This time, I roll. My trembling arm and legs have reached their limit; they can't pull any more. So-o, I roll. One rotation at a time. Collecting more muck—more filth —on the way. And, at each rotation, the bore inside my skull opens its valve and floods consciousness aside; there-fore, after each rotation, I must wait until the waters sub-side a little. I roll, nudging the holdall ahead of me, I flake out, I come round, I make one more mighty effort and shove the Tilley nearer to the door—to the head of the stairs—then I roll, again and, once more, I flake out.

There must be a million easier ways of getting from point A to point B ... but I'm incapable of using any one of the million easier ways.

Again ... how long?

Again ... God only knows.

At the top of the stairs, I wait. I have all eternity ahead of me. I can wait a few hours, rather than barbecue myself in spilled paraffin from the Tilley.

I wait, and doze. I position myself, to watch the webbed

and dirt-greyed window. Given time—given forever—dawn *has* to come.

It comes ... and it damn near *takes* forever!

CHAPTER THIRTEEN

The surf still breaks, under the dome of my skull, but it breaks less violently. It no longer rages. It no longer boils. It can, for the moment and to some degree, be controlled.

Rest, the great healer, has performed its regular miracle.

If I move slowly, carefully and smoothly I have, in part, some authority over my limbs. It is a little like the old trick of balancing a tumbler of water on the back of an outstretched hand. It needs the same amount of concentration; the same amount of steadiness. My left hand and arm remain useless—more than useless, they are a hindrance—but the rest of my body is more *mine* than it has been since I left the main downstairs room. It obeys my orders ... demanding only that those orders be given quietly, and carried out gently.

I am even able to think, with some coherence.

Why? ... for example.

What the hell has tipped the scales?

Twenty-four hours back, I was a complete man; physically, mentally, biologically, psychologically ... you name it, I was complete. I was even happy (if you can ever call what I felt 'happiness') in that I'd found Charlie; a dream come true; a wish granted. I had a complete fink for a companion—a New Scotland Yard nappy-wearer who needed nurse-maiding along a moderately normal, two-times-two pinch—but not a bad kid and a kid who, when the boom dropped, proved to be as tough as old boots.

That was a mere twenty-four hours back.

And now, this ... and I try to figure out the reason.

The wrist? The arm? Okay, that is part of it. Human flesh can take only so much; tear it, mangle it then remould it, like so much baker's dough, and the whole nervous system *has* to tighten up until it resembles a quivering hawser, on the point of snapping.

That much, then, is part of it and (for all I know) that much can trigger off the rest ... but the rest is the big part.

It is, perhaps, possible to hate too much and hate too long. To hate, and enjoy the hatred until, like freshly-whipped cream, too much of it becomes too rich a confectionery for the taste buds to drool over. For nineteen never-ending years, I've devoured hatred; I've chewed upon it with every mouthful of food, I've gulped it in with every drink and I've inhaled it with every breath I've taken. Hatred, in all its various flavours ... repugnance, gall, loathing, abhorrence, enmity, bitterness.

Bitterness ... always bitterness.

The grudge that feeds upon itself, until it consumes the whole world and becomes the only real reason for living.

And when that happens?

I know the answer to that one, too. I've *reached* the answer.

Madness ... but not a certifiable madness. Insanity ... but an insanity which, of itself, is beautifully sane.

It tips the balance of reason.

It is such a sweet fruit, and yet it turns sour at the taste but, despite the sourness, you still chew on it. You still swallow it. You still devour it ... because it's the only thing left!

And that, friend, is the complete answer to the question ... why?

Because.

I use my feet to push the holdall to the top of the stairs. Slowly—carefully—I push it forward until it topples and rolls and thumps its way down to the scullery.

Then, I follow it.

Sitting on each step at a time, edging myself gently forward until, with the slow leverage of my right arm, I can lower myself onto the step below ... balancing the tumbler on the back of my outstretched hand.

I reach the scullery in a (more or less) steady condition. I rest. I sit on the bottom step and will the noise, between my ears, to quieten a little. I concentrate my mind upon good things ... but there are so few good things, it's hardly worth the effort of concentration.

Maybe five minutes—maybe ten minutes—and I ease myself into an upright position. I sway a little, but I take the shotgun, from its position near the wall, and use it as a makeshift crutch with which to steady myself.

Slowly—like a man whose joints are wracked with rheumatoid arthritis—I edge my way into the main room. I shuffle the holdall ahead of me, with my feet.

Daylight has arrived, and the room is flooded with a cold which reaches deep into the bones; a cold which, despite my present condition, even touches *me*. It brings a quick shiver to my shoulders but (or so I pretend) it clears an odd cobweb or two from my mind. The fire is dead, and Goodwin, too, sprawls alongside death; to combat the chill of the night he has dragged the blankets from the body of the D.I., rolled himself in them, as much as his handcuffed wrist will allow, and stretched himself out on the bed.

As I enter the room, he swings his legs to the floor, keeps

a blanket across his shoulders, stares and breathes, 'God Almighty!'

The room has no mirrors ... but I know *exactly* what he means.

I shuffle the holdall to within his reach, then shuffle my way to my old position, by the wall. I lower myself, carefully—gingerly—into a sitting position, and take time off to rest after what seems to have had all the hardships of an Eiger climb.

'Ray...' he begins, then stops.

Could be there is something about the face, under all this muck. Could be there is something about the expression. Something in the eyes, other than a temporary madness.

We wait, in silence, until I have gathered enough energy, and enough will-power, to speak.

I thumb back the hammers of the twelve-bore, line the barrels onto his middle and hold my fingers ready.

I croak, 'Open it up, Charlie. Let's see what ten thousand looks like.'

He slips the blanket from his shoulders, stands up from the bed and pulls the holdall nearer. He works the zip and, like a maw opening up, the mouth of the holdall gapes and bundles of fives and singles threaten to spew out onto the flagstones. Money. A lot of money ... even in this inflated age, a lot of money.

'What's it going to buy you, Charlie?' I whisper.

'I thought, maybe...' Once more, he breaks off, before the sentence is complete.

'What?'

'An even chance,' he says, softly.

'The same chance you gave *him*?' I glance at the dead D.I.

'You, and me, Ray.'

'We're back to first names, again,' I mock.

'For old times' sake.'

'What old times?'

'We had some good times. Once.'

'Yeah.' I almost nod, but remember not to, in time. I rasp, 'Napoleon had some good screws from Josephine ... but not after Elba.'

'Ten G. I think that's worth an even break, Cameron.'

'For the good times?'

'Uhuh.'

'For all the booze-ups?'

'We had a few.'

'For all the tarts we shafted?'

'Them, too.'

'Charlie,' I sigh, 'you have suddenly become endowed with a very long memory. A very *convenient* memory.'

'It happened.'

I almost laugh. Almost! But the tidal wave inside my head races the laughter to the post, and beats it, by a nose. Therefore, I do not laugh. Instead, I close my eyes and fight back the flood of noise and, with it, the spinning darkness.

I open my eyes, and whisper, 'What's it like, outside, Charlie?'

'Outside?'

'The weather?'

'Oh!' A gleam of hope glints, for a moment, in his good eye.

'What's it like?'

'Fine. The sun's gathering strength.'

'Thawing?'

'Yeah ... thawing.'

The surf pounds, and expends its strength on the shingle of my mind, with the monotony of a trip-hammer. I fight to ignore it; to pretend it isn't there; to concentrate my whole attention upon this single moment ... this one bastard ... this accidental, but perfect, situation ...

'An even break,' I murmur.

'That's all I ask,' he says, eagerly.

I pretend to give it thought, then say, 'Back to the bed, Charlie. Sit down.'

He sits down.

'I leave you the money,' he urges.

'That goes without saying.'

'Ten thousand, Cameron. You can do a lot with ten thousand.'

'If I can keep it.'

'Hide it. Tell 'em the tale. Tell 'em I took it with me.'

'Hide it?' I try for just the right amount of contempt.

'In one of the out-buildings. In the old tractor shed. There's a hundred places ... till you can come and collect it.'

He thinks I'm crazy. He *really* thinks I'm crazy! In my condition—fighting this noise, wrestling against unconsciousness ... and he's trying to con me into believing I can walk out and hide the holdall.

Charlie, boy, you can't con an old cop. You'll learn ... the hardest way of all.

So-o, here comes the counter-con.

I say, 'How do I know?'

'What?'

'That you'll keep your side of the deal?'

'What the hell?' He puts on a look of surprise.

'You're a cunning devil, Charlie. You always were.'

He leans forward a little, fills his voice with mock-

honesty, and says, 'I want freedom, Cameron. That's all
... freedom. Why else would I hole out in a place like
this? Just help me. That's all I ask. Let me walk out of
that door. Give me that much of a break—no more ...
and you're a rich man.'

'Rich?' I try a smile for size, but it doesn't quite fit.

'Ten thousand isn't breadcrumbs.'

'No-o,' I agree.

'Most men wouldn't hesitate.'

I watch his smashed-up face and, behind my eyes, my
brain is working like the clappers, trying to hold the
shards of my splintering mind together. To *think*—such
a little thing ... but that's all I'm working to do.

He says, 'What the hell has the police force done for
you?'

'Not much.'

'What is it? Detective constable?'

'That's all.'

'And this young pup? Detective inspector?'

'*Was*, Charlie.'

'You're as good. Better.'

'Maybe.'

'So, why not?'

'It's a good argument, Charlie. The best, so far.'

'They're *all* good arguments, Cameron.'

I give him some silence. That's the trick; to know when
to talk, and to know when *not* to talk; to let the sucker
convince *himself*; to let *him* do as much work as possible.

He thinks I'm on the topple.

He says, 'Take it, Cameron. Don't be a mug all your
life. Call it winning the pools. Let me walk out of here,
and take the jackpot.'

'And me?' I ask.

'Who'll know?'

'No—I don't mean that ... I mean *me*. I need a medic.'

'Okay.' He nods. The pay-off line is coming up. The oh-so-clever, would-be sucker-bait is on its way. He says, 'Two hours. That's all. The snow's going. I should be well clear, in two hours. Two hours, and the first kiosk I see, I use. I'll telephone—I'll not give my name ... but I'll tell 'em where you are, and that you need an ambulance. Agreed?'

Now comes the timing. The timing has to be perfect. Not too eager, not too reluctant ... just right.

I count fifty, slowly.

Then, I ease the hammers of the twelve-bore down, lay the shotgun across my legs and fumble in my pocket. I find the handcuff key. I toss it towards the bed then, as a natural place to rest my hand, I return my fingers to the shotgun ... to within an inch of the trigger-guard.

Charlie's eye never leaves me, as he stands up from the bed and picks up the key. Slowly—almost unbelievingly—he uses the key and releases the bracelet from his wrist. He leaves the key in the opened bracelet, and leaves the handcuffs dangling from the ironwork of the bed.

He glances down at the holdall—at all those notes—and gives a quick, lop-sided grin. Almost of cynical regret. Almost as if he *isn't* contemplating coming back to collect his hard-earned loot.

He takes a deep breath, then murmurs, 'Thanks Cameron. I'll—er—I'll take the kid's coat ... if you don't mind.'

'Be my guest.'

He takes the mohair coat from the bed—from where it has been used to give extra warmth to its owner, before its owner was beyond extra warmth—and threads his arms through the sleeves. The coat isn't a bad fit.

184

My fingers have moved. They are now nursing the twin triggers of the twelve-bore.

Once more, he looks at the money, then says, 'Spend it well, Cameron. It's been earned ... don't waste it.'

'It'll be used,' I assure him.

He steps over the holdall, walks to the door and raises the sneck.

I snap back the hammers of the twelve-bore and he freezes, with the door no more than three inches open.

In a very threatening voice, I say, 'Don't look round, Charlie. Don't even take a chance ... you're dead, if you try.'

He talks to the door.

The rusty-hinge of a voice has a tremor in it, as he says, 'What the hell is this, Cameron? What sort of double-cross ...?'

'I'll talk. You listen. You need to know things ... you need to know one hell of a lot of things, before you go.'

'Okay. I'm listening.'

'Just don't look round ... that's all.'

'Okay.'

He stays perfectly still. Facing the slightly opened door, and with his hand still resting on the latch.

I force myself to forget everything north of the eye-brows. I concentrate upon what I'm saying. Every word. I concentrate on keeping the barrels steady, and lined on the small of his back.

I say, 'You'd have liked your kid, Charlie. He was a dummy ... but he was a nice kid. He was full of love. Love, for all mankind. He might even have loved the bastard who fathered him. I think you'd have liked him.'

The muscles at the nape of his neck move, slightly. As if they've been touched by an ice-pack.

I say, 'That's why you split, Charlie. That's why you blew. She was in the family way ... and you didn't want to know. I took her on the rebound. I made her—y'know ... "honest". But it was the rebound. I didn't kid myself ... she even called the kid after the name of its father.

'That didn't stop me from being crazy about her. I married her ... I was very proud to marry her. I was even proud when her kid—*your* kid—became my son ... even though he was only my son according to law.'

'I—I didn't know. If I'd...'

'You're a liar, Charlie. You knew. She *told* you. She told *me* ... she was too honest a person not to tell me. You knew ... that's why you skipped town.

'That was okay, Charlie. I didn't hold it against you. I was even grateful. You gave me a damn good wife ... and a son, as a bonus. But the son was a little like his father, Charlie. Crazy. Without brains. Without know-how. And she wouldn't accept that. *She wouldn't accept it.* And it was killing her, inch at a time. She was going nuts ... and something had to be done.'

I pause, gather myself for that last sprint to the tape, then say, 'I loved them both, Charlie. Both! But, I loved her even more than I loved him ... fractionally more. Only fractionally more ... but more. So-o, what else? When I looked in the mirror. When I saw him there, playing in the drive. When I *could* have braked. What else? I closed my eyes, and kept right on reversing. *I killed your dummy, Charlie.* Deliberately. I killed him, deliberately, because it seemed the only way out. The only humane way. The only answer. Your kid, Charlie ... *I murdered him.*'

His head moves a little. It droops forward. Maybe from shame—maybe from shock—maybe from an acceptance of the inevitable ... with a bastard like this, who knows?

My voice is just about bursting with bitter memory, as I say, 'And for nothing, Charlie. For nothing! The horse-laugh. The "Cameron Special". In all my life, I've looked up to two people. I killed one, and drove the other into a looney-house.

'As far as she's concerned, Charlie's still alive. Little Charlie is still around ... even though he's only a teddy bear she won't part with. That's the horse-laugh. That I got away with murder ... but I didn't get away with punishment. The punishment was something I couldn't dodge. And, buster! That punishment ... no man *knows*.

'But you, Charlie. You get away with everything. Every damn thing. You're the boy who never holds the lemon. Never!

'You know what hatred is, Charlie? Hatred? The real McCoy? I'm talking about hatred, Charlie. *Hatred!* Not dislike. Not not getting along with somebody. I'm talking about something bone-deep. Soul-deep. It's like Old Man Ford's original Model T. It comes in any colour you fancy ... but always black. There's nothing like it, for keeping a man moving forward. For keeping him alive, and coming. And, Charlie, you've got it. From me, to you. Every ounce I've ever been able to gather ... and every ounce of it black!'

Again I paused then, when I speak, my voice is a hoarse whisper which carries all the loathing of far too many years.

I say, 'You're not a man, Charlie. You're a louse ... and that's why. That's why—because you're a louse— you're going to get it just where you deserve it ... in the back!'

The triggers are already fully depressed. All I have to do is lift my thumb from the hammers.

The twin blasts lift the top of my skull and send the waters roaring in, to drown me. I fight to retain consciousness long enough to know ... long enough to be *certain*.

The punch of the buckshot smashes him into the door—slams the door closed—then bounces him back, towards me. He lands in my lap, rag-doll limp and very dead. A lot of blood, and some of his guts, spill out and soak my trousers.

Odd ... I feel neither remorse nor satisfaction.

I feel nothing.

As the blackness takes over, I feel like Charlie ... *dead*!

CHAPTER FOURTEEN

In the top office of Police Headquarters, the Chief Constable made clucking noises with his tongue, and shook his head.

He said, 'New Scotland Yard are getting impatient. They want a full report, as soon as possible.'

The A.C.C. (Crime) scowled his displeasure, and growled, 'They've already had a full report ... all we know. We've got the man, we've got the money. After that, it's all guesswork.'

'They've a dead inspector. They want an explanation.'

'We've a dead D.C.,' countered the A.C.C. (Crime). 'The pathologist says the D.I. died some considerable time before Cameron and Goodwin. Reconstruction—what little reconstruction we can come up with—suggests the D.I. stopped a twelve-bore blast, in the legs, before he even entered the place. That makes Cameron something of a hero. It makes *their* man something of an idiot.'

'I should play that down,' advised the C.C.

'What about Cameron?' asked the A.C.C. (Crime).

'What about him?' The C.C. looked puzzled.

'At a guess, he was stopping Goodwin from making a run for it. His condition—the filth on his clothes and face —the filth on the holdall ... they don't leave much room for doubt. More reconstruction, if you like. But, it seems obvious, Cameron crawled upstairs and retrieved the money. Equally obviously, he was in pain at the time.'

'Then, what?' asked the Chief Constable, with a wry smile.

'Goodwin tried to break arrest. Cameron shot him. That's how I read it.'

'Really?'

The A.C.C. (Crime) rubbed his jaw, then said, 'I'd say Cameron deserves some sort of posthumous pat on the back.'

'Not the Queen's Police Medal, for God's sake,' said the C.C., sternly.

'Oh, no ... not that. Not *that*.'

'Too many imponderables.'

'Ye-es ... I suppose so,' agreed the A.C.C. (Crime).

'That wrist, for example.'

'I know.' The A.C.C. (Crime) nodded, sagely. 'Heaven only knows how he came to have *that* injury.'

'And the fact that the handcuffs were unlocked.'

'I know.'

'With the key still in them.'

'Quite.'

'Far too many imponderables.'

'Quite,' repeated the A.C.C. (Crime).

'Cause of death,' mused the Chief Constable. 'What is it? A combination of shock, exposure and exhaustion ... that covers a few square miles of ground.'

'Could mean anything,' agreed the A.C.C. (Crime).

The Chief Constable fiddled with papers, on his desk, impatiently.

He said, 'When's the funeral?'

'Cremation. Day after tomorrow.'

'Who'll be there?'

'I've organised a uniformed escort, for the coffin ...'

'Good.'

'...and, as far as I can make out, the only civilian mourners will be his wife, his sister and his brother-in-law.'

'His—er—*wife*?' The C.C. looked startled. 'I thought she was ... y'know.'

The A.C.C. (Crime) said, 'She's much improved. So I'm told. Back to normal, almost. More or less on terms with reality again.'

'Good. I'm pleased ... but—er—this little lot won't have helped.'

'I don't think she minds.' The A.C.C. (Crime) smiled. 'Cameron hasn't visited her for years. As far as she's concerned, he's just a name ... she doesn't really remember him.'

'Y'know,' observed the C.C., 'some men are out-and-out bastards.'

'Indeed, they are,' agreed the A.C.C. (Crime), feelingly.

The Chief Constable said, 'Let me know the exact time of the cremation. I'll nip along, and salute the coffin ... that should satisfy everybody.'

'I'll do that, sir.'

'Oh, and—er—concoct some sort of a report for New Scotland Yard. Smooth 'em down a bit. Tell 'em how sorry we are ... and what a bloody fine policeman their man was.'

PRODUCTION
EDITO-SERVICE S.A., GENEVA

PRINTED IN ITALY